Joe handed the little girl a bat.

"Try to hit the ball off the tee," he said. Amy swung the bat, completely missing the ball. When she started to walk away, Joe pulled her back, trying to be patient.

"Don't give up now!" he urged. "You just need a little work, that's all. Straighten that arm and lower it a bit. You're doing fine. Now, try it again."

Wishbone watched Amy hunch over the bat, then swing with all her might. This time she struck  Joe squarely in the hip with the bat. Joe doubled over, wincing in pain while the little girl giggled.

Wishbone yelped in sympathy. "It's a strike! But somehow I don't think it's the kind of hit Joe wants."

Other books in the
Adventures of **wishbone**™ series:

Be a Wolf!

Salty Dog

The Prince and the Pooch

Robinhound Crusoe*

Hunchdog of Notre Dame*

Digging Up the Past*

*coming soon

THE PRINCE
and the
POOCH

by Caroline Leavitt
Based on the teleplay by Mo Rocca
Inspired by *The Prince and the Pauper* by Mark Twain
WISHBONE™ created by Rick Duffield

Big Red Chair Books™, *A Division of Lyrick Publishing*™

This book is a work of fiction. The characters, incidents, and dialogues are products of the author's imagination and are not to be construed as real. Any resemblance to actual events or persons, living or dead, is entirely coincidental.

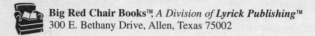 **Big Red Chair Books**™, *A Division of Lyrick Publishing*™
300 E. Bethany Drive, Allen, Texas 75002

©1997 Big Feats! Entertainment

Edited by Kevin Ryan

Copy edited by Jonathon Brodman

Cover design and interior illustrations by Lyle Miller

Cover concept by Kathryn Yingling

Wishbone photograph by Carol Kaelson

ISBN: 1-57064-196-X

First printing: July 1997

10 9 8 7 6 5 4 3 2

To my two favorite guys, with love—

my husband, Jeff, and my son, Max

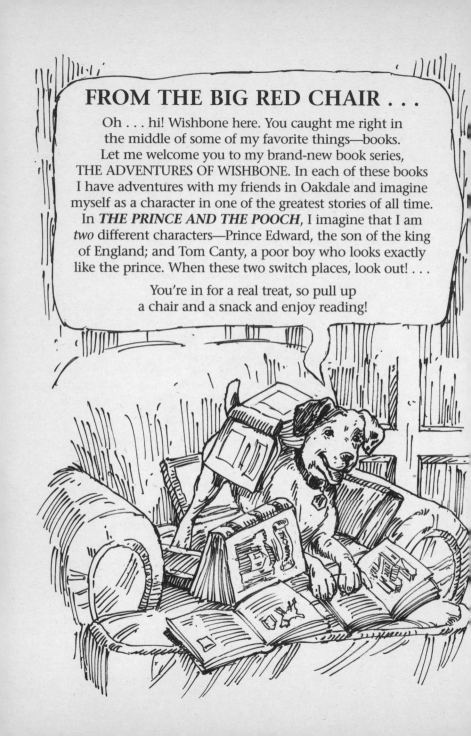

FROM THE BIG RED CHAIR . . .

Oh . . . hi! Wishbone here. You caught me right in
the middle of some of my favorite things—books.
Let me welcome you to my brand-new book series,
THE ADVENTURES OF WISHBONE. In each of these books
I have adventures with my friends in Oakdale and imagine
myself as a character in one of the greatest stories of all time.
In **THE PRINCE AND THE POOCH**, I imagine that I am
two different characters—Prince Edward, the son of the king
of England; and Tom Canty, a poor boy who looks exactly
like the prince. When these two switch places, look out! . . .

You're in for a real treat, so pull up
a chair and a snack and enjoy reading!

Chapter One

Ah! A brand-new morning in Oakdale! Wishbone got his last licks in on a particularly tasty breakfast of kibble. Then he trotted behind Ellen to the front door. "I hate to eat and run," he apologized to Ellen. "But never fear, I'll be back for my mid-morning snack." He scratched at the door. "The call of the wild, you know!" he said.

"Here you go, Wishbone." Ellen opened the door.

"Thank you, Ellen." Wishbone stepped outside, breathing as deeply as he could. "Ah! The Great Outdoors and the first sniff of the day!" he said.

Wishbone instantly knew something was up. The air was filled with a delicious new blend of scents. There was fresh-cut grass that he ached to roll in. He smelled flowers he wanted to romp through. He smelled bones crying out to be unburied. He even caught the scent of a steak barbecuing from two blocks away!

"A breakfast barbecue!" cried Wishbone. "How innovative! How creative! How delicious! I like a person who doesn't stand on ceremony. Let's see, who's the host?" Wishbone said, taking a deeper sniff. "Lime aftershave—why, that's Mr. Pruitt. This must be part of that new high-protein diet he was telling Ellen about yesterday." Wishbone stood up on his hind legs and sniffed again. "Grilled ham! I smell mustard! And—yes, yes—he's flipping the ham!" Wishbone was so excited that he flipped head over paws himself. "Mr. Pruitt knows I like protein as much as the next pooch. My invitation to his feast must have gotten lost in the mail," Wishbone decided. "But he doesn't stand on ceremony. I bet I could just drop on by. Mr. Pruitt seems to be missing only one ingredient in his feast. I know what it is, too—a dog!"

Ellen bent down and ruffled Wishbone's fur. "You're sure excited, but I can't say I blame you. Look at this gorgeous day!"

Wishbone forgot the barbecue for a moment. He looked up at the sky, which was as bright a color of blue as his food bowl. Suddenly, not just his tail but his whole body wagged with excitement.

"Can it be!" he exclaimed. "Can it be? Yes! Yes! Spring is here! In the air and in my step. It's apparent in so many ways. Just look over there. Wanda's flowers are blooming."

Wishbone perked up his ears at the soft *thwack!* of a ball slapping into a leather baseball glove. He followed the sound to its source. Just down the street, Joe, Samantha, and David were tossing a softball back and forth.

"And, of course," Wishbone said, "everyone's enjoying America's favorite pastime. Play ball!"

He trotted toward the players.

"You know," he said, "I think that my cheerleading days are over. I am ready to play. Yes, sir, this dog has got bases to run, home runs to hit, and ground balls to fetch. This pup is up for anything!"

He was almost to the game when the kids suddenly stopped playing.

"Let's take a break," Joe said. He threw the ball to Samantha.

"Hey, hey, wait a minute!" Wishbone said. "Throw it to me!"

All three of the kids walked slowly back to the street. Samantha tossed the ball lazily up and down. Sometimes, she passed it to David, who threw it back to her.

"Yoo-hoo! Ball to Wishbone!" Wishbone called. He put himself directly in Sam's path. She tossed the ball to Joe. "Nobody ever listens to the dog," Wishbone lamented. He fell into step with Joe and his friends.

"Hi, Wishbone," Joe said, bending to ruffle Wishbone's fur.

"A little to the left," Wishbone urged. "Ah! That's the spot!"

Joe turned back to his friends, looking disgusted. "I'm telling you, David, that game was so terrible. The coach should have had us play man to man."

Samantha pushed back her baseball cap. "Come on, Joe. The game's over," she said. "Forget about it."

"Yes," Wishbone agreed, nudging Joe's leg. "Get your mind off it and think about something else . . . something less stressful, perhaps. A game with a player you can always count on. If you're talking one-on-one, how about a round of fetch with yours truly?"

The group passed Mr. Barnes. He was practicing his golf swing on his front lawn. Wishbone eyed the golf ball, which looked small and white and absolutely delicious.

Now, that's what I call bite-sized! Wishbone thought, edging in closer.

Mr. Barnes saw the kids and grinned. "Hey, what's up, guys? How are you doing, Wishbone?" He bent and scooped up the golf ball from under Wishbone's nose and put it into his pocket. "Sorry, fellow, but I've lost one too many golf balls to you. They all somehow wind up buried in Wanda's garden."

"Hey, hey, don't be so hasty," Wishbone said. "Can we talk about this, maybe negotiate something?"

Joe shook his head, still upset. "Mr. Barnes, we could have gone all the way in the game! Coach Menendez let us down. That's all there is to it."

Mr. Barnes shrugged his shoulders. "Well, what can I say? Being coach is never easy."

Joe looked surprised. "Sure it is! If I were coaching, we could have won the game. Any good player can coach."

A smile played across Mr. Barnes's face. "Is that so? It's that simple?"

"Of course. Simple as pie."

"Joe, be careful," Wishbone warned. "Take it from me, things that look simple—the perfect bark, the perfect fetch—are sometimes the hardest."

Mr. Barnes smiled again. "Well, Joe, I'd be willing to give you a chance to prove it—you know, experience firsthand how the other half lives. Experience is a great teacher."

"Uh-oh," Samantha said.

"What do you mean?" Joe asked, clearly intrigued.

"Well," said Mr. Barnes, "Emily's T-ball season just started and I need an assistant coach—just for a few practice sessions until we play our first game." He leaned against his white picket fence and waited. "So, what do you say, Coach?"

David and Samantha exchanged doubtful glances.

Wishbone wound himself around Joe's legs. "Stand up for what you want, Joe. I'll support you." Joe shifted his weight suddenly, tripping over the dog.

"Wishbone!" he said, righting himself.

"Whoops! Sorry, got just a mite overenthusiastic, there," said Wishbone, stepping back a bit. "I don't know my own strength since I took all of those dog aerobic classes. More pounce to the ounce."

"You don't know what you're in for. My sister Emily and her team can be really tough on a coach," David said to Joe. Joe was too excited to listen.

"You've got a deal," Joe told Mr. Barnes.

"Well," said Wishbone doubtfully, "I'm not so sure that playing fetch isn't a better idea, but if this is what you really want . . . okay. Count this hound in, too. Let me just check my busy schedule." He scratched, trying to think. "Let's see . . . chasing cars is on Saturday morning, digging up the flowerbeds I like to save for Sunday . . . barking at cats is a Friday sort of thing . . . and, of course, there are those breakfast barbecues coming up all the time—but, you know, I think I could pencil this in!"

Joe held out his hand and Mr. Barnes shook it enthusiastically.

"Let's *all* shake on it!" said Wishbone, lifting his paw.

Ah! A wish has been granted! Joe the player becomes Joe the coach. It reminds me of the story *The Prince and the Pauper*, written by Mark Twain in 1882. It's about two young boys living in sixteenth-century England. The boys, just like Joe, also had their chance to get what they wanted—or what they *thought* they wanted—when they traded places!

Chapter Two

Wishbone loved the story *The Prince and the Pauper* so much that he imagined he was *both* of the main characters in Twain's book. He dreamed that he was the beloved little Prince Edward. Edward was a purebred dressed in glowing silks and fancy satins. He lived in the lap of luxury. Best of all, he was about to inherit the throne from his father, King Henry VIII. Wishbone also fantasized that he was the ragged pauper, Tom Canty. Tom was a mongrel. His poor life was filled with beatings and hunger. Tom's dearest dream was to see the prince.

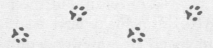

Holy cats! Imagining myself as two different people in one great story—that's really shaking up the tale! You know, pretending to be someone else is so much fun that even the writer Mark Twain himself did it. His real name was Samuel Clemens. However, he wrote his books under the fake name—or what we in literary circles call the *pen name*—Mark Twain. The words "Mark Twain" are a water-measurement term from Clemens's time when he piloted a riverboat. It means "four fathoms deep"—one fathom being equal to six feet.

All Wishbone had to do was shut his eyes. Then he could see and smell what sixteenth-century London must have been like. It was a time of both great poverty and great wealth. The city streets where the pauper lived were narrow, crooked, unpaved, dirty, and caked with mud. The noisy crowds of people who lived there were equally unwashed. They always fought or shouted or tried to steal what little they could. There was almost nothing to eat. Clothing was so ragged and faded from use and washing that you could no longer make out any of its colors. The houses were built of wood and painted red or blue or black. The paint was always chipping, and the rickety houses were always dangerously in need of repair. But the palace, where the prince lived, was made of marble and gold, and it sparkled with jewels. It was wonderfully quiet and smelled of the rarest perfumes. The hundreds of servants and courtiers—attendants at the royal court—were all polite and well-bred. There was so much mouth-watering food! Why, you would need an industrial-strength doggie bag to cart it away!

The palace! Who wouldn't want to live the life of luxury in the palace! Wishbone knew the pauper surely did. Wishbone began to really concentrate. Suddenly, he imagined he was Tom again, a bold young pup dressed in tattered rags. He was making his way paw by paw past London Bridge. He headed toward the palace gates, where Prince Edward was due to appear any minute.

Ears pinned back, nose to the air, Tom pushed himself through the rough crowd. Even from far back, he could see the palace. It was two stories high, reaching to the sky. It was golden and gleaming in the bright sunlight. Tom's eyes grew large with wonder and delight. He felt a thrill run up along his fur. Granite lion statues bordered the palace entrance, and silken red banners hung from the windows and waved in the breeze. The palace was set back in a huge courtyard lined with trees and flowers. Splendid carriages drawn by snow-white horses arrived at the gate. Magnificent lords and ladies stepped out of them.

Tom could hardly contain himself from barking with glee. Back in his neighborhood, he had often heard stories of the prince and the palace. They were wonderful tales. Sometimes in his part of the city he would have hard days of sitting up and begging. Often he had nothing to show for his efforts but a hungry belly and no one to scratch it for him. What made him feel better was to dream of being a prince.

At home Tom slept on a patch of filthy straw. How grand it would be to sleep on a silk pillow like a prince! He wore rough, torn burlap. How marvelous to wear satin like a prince! Everyone barked orders at him. If he were a prince, he would bark the orders. "I'd make a great prince," he kept telling everyone. "Everyone would do my bidding when I did so little as to simply whine in my sleep!" When he told these tales, everyone laughed at him, but Tom didn't mind.

He tried to find out everything he could about princes, especially Prince Edward. He knew that the prince's father, King Henry VIII, was very ill, and was not expected to live much longer. Edward, the very same age as Tom, could inherit the throne any minute. There would be a coronation ceremony to crown Edward king. It was something most people never had a chance to see in their entire lifetime. Tom had only read and dreamed about such a spectacle. "Such an event would be more wonderful than anything!" Tom cried. The books said that everyone in London would turn out for a coronation. The streets would be filled with music and dancing. All the people would put on their very finest clothing. Dukes and duchesses and all sorts of other royalty would appear. The common people, like Tom, could see them. Maybe he could even get close enough to touch them!

I'd make a great king, Tom thought. *But if I can't be the king, the next best thing would be to see the boy who will be! And I shall see Prince Edward!*

But Tom wasn't the only one trying to catch a glimpse of the young prince. It seemed that all of London had shown up. Crowds of people laughed and cheered and clapped one another on the back. Food and drink were passed from hand to hand. The mob was filthy and foul-smelling and rude. They crowded up toward the golden gates of the palace, roughly shoving anyone who got in their way.

Tom was determined. He wagged his body this way and that. He pushed his front paws right up against the gate. Occasionally, he jumped, snatching a breath of fresh air. A fierce-looking soldier stood guard, wearing a suit of armor so fierce and shiny and silvery that Tom could see his own poor reflection mirrored back to him. Burrs were stuck along his hindquarters. His coat was matted and dull. *Not exactly bright-eyed and bushy-tailed, am I?* he thought.

"Step aside, you're in my way!" someone shouted, standing directly in front of Tom. Tom struggled up on his hind legs for a better position.

"Please, please, people!" Tom begged. "Suffer a

young pauper to see the prince, and then my life might seem less wretched! I've dreamed and dreamed of what it might be like to be the prince myself. All I want is one little look!"

Tom nosed closer. Suddenly, he spied something that made his heart pound. There was the prince! Prince Edward! His coat was so glossy that it seemed to reflect light.

"He's got elegance nailed down front, back, and on his hindquarters," Tom whispered, catching sight of the prince's manicured paws. Around his neck he wore a diamond-studded collar. He was dressed in shining silks and satins. He wore a magnificent purple plumed hat and shining gold ID tags. "Now that's what I call a license to thrill!" Tom said. "It is he!" he cried. "The prince! So regal! So royal! So noble! So clean!" He strained his eyes. "And so very far away. I must have a better look."

He was about to make a gravity-defying leap. Suddenly, the soldier slapped Tom across the head, striking him with the flat of his hand. Tom yelped in surprise. "Mind thy manners, thou young beggar!" the soldier warned.

Tom's misery attracted the attention of the crowd. The mob jeered and laughed at Tom, but the young prince noticed the soldier's show of force with royal displeasure. He came forward, whiskers bristling, and addressed the soldier with great anger. "How dare you treat this boy like that! Open the gate and let him in!"

Reluctantly, the soldier opened the gate and the crowd parted. Tom couldn't believe his eyes! The prince was looking kindly at him.

"Thou looks tired and hungry. Come with me," the prince said.

Tom looked back at the soldier, who frowned at him. "See ya later, big guy!" he said. "Guess your bark is worse than your bite."

Tom trotted after the prince. He couldn't believe it. He was in the palace! It was more splendid in reality than even in his wildest dreams. They entered a golden hall that seemed twice the size of Tom's entire neighborhood of Offal Court. Tom stood up on his hind legs to see the ceiling. It was twenty feet high and painted with a colorful mural of angels flying through a bright blue sky.

"Wow!" he exclaimed, coming back down to the ground with a thump.

The whole room was filled with servants, dressed in blue satin. As soon as they spied Edward, they whispered, "The prince comes! The prince comes!" They all bowed deeply in front of Edward and Tom.

"Come on," Edward said, leading Tom up a polished wood stairway. There were so many steps that Tom began to count them. He stopped counting only when he had reached the number one hundred. The second floor was no less splendid than the first. The walls were all covered in blue silk. On either side of the hallway was magnificent room after magnificent room after magnificent room. Not only did these rooms all look different to Tom, but they smelled different, too. There was a red room that had the scent of wildflowers. A blue room smelled of clear lakes. There was even a room covered in green wallpaper that smelled like a grassy field. Tom had to stop and sniff at it twice because it made him ache to roll in the grass.

Edward took Tom to a huge hallway where the walls were covered in blue velvet. The marble floors were so smooth and shiny that he skidded across them. Bracing his paws, he tried to slow down. Even so, he tumbled into a heap. Tom tucked his tail under and tried again, skidding to a halt at the end of the hallway. "I guess getting there is half the fun!"

He was at the entrance of a great room, when half a dozen attendants suddenly appeared.

"Wow! They come out of nowhere, don't they?" Tom said.

"Your Highness!" the attendants said all together, bowing deeply. Edward lifted one paw and waved them away.

"Come on," he said to Tom, taking him into a sumptuous room that had a soft red carpet set upon the floor. The prince perched upon a green velvet chair in front of Tom and motioned for him to come forward. "Please be seated," Prince Edward said. "What is thy name?"

"Tom Canty, sir."

"And where do you live, Tom Canty?"

"Offal Court. It isn't much, but it's home."

"Offal Court," repeated the prince. "Why, I have never heard of such a place."

"I share a room with my family."

"And servants?" asked the prince.

Tom laughed. "No servants."

"Who dresses you, then? And who makes your meals? And who feeds and washes you and gives you your flea bath?"

"Why, I dress myself," said Tom. "And I sleep on what straw no one else has claimed for the night. I wash myself when I can find some water. As for meals—well, it's catch as catch can, Your Highness. Table scraps . . . that sort of thing."

The prince studied the pauper with growing concern. "Tell me, why art thou so frail?"

Tom gave the prince a hangdog look. "Oh, lousy food and beatings."

"Beatings?" The prince looked surprised.

"What can I say? It's a dog-eat-dog world out there, Prince. You must understand."

The prince seemed puzzled. "Yes," he said slowly, "I suppose I should." He looked at Tom. "Tell me, hast thou any pleasures?"

Tom brightened a bit. "Some, sir. My life is not all bad, mind you. We have Punch-and-Judy puppet shows. There are monkeys! And there are plays!"

"Plays! How wonderful! Tell me more!"

"Well, in the summer, sir, we swim in the river. I do a mean dog paddle!"

The prince began to get excited. "Yes!"

"And we dive in the pond!"

The prince leaned closer to Tom. "Oh, yes, continue!" he begged.

"When we get really excited, we start to do a tumble!" Tom leaped into the air and flipped head over paws.

The delighted prince cried, "Go on! Go on!"

"Well, we sing and we dance! And the mud!" Tom cried. "The mud, Prince! We roll in the mud!"

Tom turned around and around across the marble floor, chasing his tail, until the prince could no longer contain himself. He leaped down from his throne and romped right along with Tom.

"Let the good times roll!" Tom said with delight.

The two rolled like whirling tops, their tails wagging, until they were both breathless.

"But you, Your Highness, have a wonderful life here, don't you?" Tom asked. "You don't have to take orders from anyone, do you?"

"Well, for now, I obey my father, whom I love dearly," Edward admitted. "But one day they'll put the crown on my head. I'll be king, and then I will take orders from no one. I will be able to do whatever I like. I can make kibble the national food if I want to."

"Oh, that would be wonderful!"

Edward nodded and then looked a little worried. "My father is sick. I know some people don't like him and say his laws are cruel. But I would rather he be well and healthy. I can wait for my coronation."

"Imagine what it will be like when you are

crowned!" Tom said, his eyes growing large with wonder. "I will be there. Nothing will keep me from attending this next coronation! Not rain or snow or the heaviest leash!" Tom looked wistful and rubbed one paw across his face. "Your life sounds wonderful to me."

The prince shook his head. "Well, sometimes it is. But *your* life sounds like fun to me now. If I could just have your life for a day! Maybe I could even give up the crown and my pedigree."

"And if I could have your life for one day!" Tom said with great yearning. "Just once I would like to look like Best of Show."

The prince grinned. Then he started to do a most remarkable thing. He began to take off his fine royal attire and set it on the floor.

"What are you doing?" the pauper asked.

"Come on," said the prince. "Take off your rags and put on my splendid attire. We will switch places just for a bit. We can change back again before anyone knows of it. It will be great fun! It's a wonderful game of pretend! You do like games, don't you?"

Tom hesitated, glancing down at his humble attire. "Well, I like fetch, and I'm great at chase-the-cat, if I do say so myself." He looked doubtfully at Edward. "Are you sure you want to do this? My clothes are a little flea-bitten, I'm afraid."

Edward laughed. "I've had my shots."

"Well," Tom said, "maybe I will try on your clothes just for size. What could it hurt?"

They quickly dressed and then the prince led Tom to a large gold-framed mirror. Each one stared at his reflection.

"Oh, my goodness!" Tom cried. "We're alike to the nose and whisker!"

"Upon my word, young Tom," said the prince, "you look like me, and I look like you. We might even be mistaken for each other."

"We might, indeed!" Tom fingered his fancy new suit of clothing. "But you have a much better tailor." He squinted at the mirror and smoothed his rough fur. "You have a better class of fleas. Your coat also stands heads and tails above mine."

The prince began to laugh. He surveyed Tom and suddenly his laughter stopped and he frowned. "And you have that awful bruise the soldier gave you."

"Oh, it's nothing," Tom said, but the prince shook his head.

"It certainly *is* something," he assured Tom. "And I intend to do something about it. You're a fine fellow, Tom Canty. Please wait here for me a moment. I must have a word with that brutal guard. Then we'll fetch the royal vet."

"Oh, all right," Tom said, sitting on the velvet chair. "But hurry back, Prince!"

The prince left the palace. Since he was so well disguised in the pauper's rags, he went right past the other courtiers. They didn't give this tattered young pup a second glance! Edward sped from the palace and approached the guard at the front gate.

Edward surveyed the crowd. *Well, this is a mob scene, isn't it?* he thought. He looked at the guard who had struck Tom. Then he drew himself up as regally as possible. "Say, you there. I must express my disappointment with your behavior."

The guard looked at the prince's ragged clothes and laughed in ridicule. "So, back from the palace already, are you, you little ruffian? What happened, did the prince tire of you and kick you out?"

"You dare to laugh in the presence of the future king!" the prince cried. He was so fired with anger that even his cold nose began to warm. The guard opened up the gate and roughly grabbed the prince by the scruff of his neck. He flung Edward down hard onto his front paws into the midst of the jeering crowd just outside the gate.

"Come back soon, you beggar!" the guard said mockingly.

"What are you doing? I am no beggar! Do I look as if I need to beg for money or squeaky toys or table scraps? I am the prince of Wales!" shouted the prince, but no one listened to him. Instead, he found himself pushed farther and farther into the unruly mob.

They took great glee in his discomfort. "All hail the prince of Wales!" they yelled with scorn.

"Oh, the people salute Your Gracious Highness!"

the guard called out sarcastically, thumbing his nose. "Be gone, thou piece of rubbish!"

The crowd stormed around the frightened prince. Soon, he was carried farther and farther from the palace and the life he knew, and was plunged deeper and deeper into a strange new world that he had never experienced.

Boy, wanting a taste of the pauper's life doesn't seem like such a crowning achievement for the poor prince right now, does it?

Let's wag on over back to the palace. I wonder if the pauper is finding *his* visit richly rewarding.

Chapter Three

Wishbone closed his eyes and fantasized that *he* was Tom now. He was having the grandest time of his young life playing at being the prince. He studied and admired himself in the palace mirror from every angle.

"You handsome dog!" Tom complimented his reflection. He turned this way and that in front of the glass. He couldn't stop touching the rich velvet of his clothing, the smooth silk that rippled against his fur. Even his fleas stood up and took notice. "If everyone at Offal Court could just see me now!" he exclaimed. "I can sit up on the furniture without so much as a frown to block my way!" He romped around the grand hall with a flourish. Then he sat in each one of the velvet chairs in the room and pretended to hold court, motioning to an imaginary group of courtiers. "My lords and ladies!" he exclaimed. "Tonight we shall dine every hour on the hour. Snacks are the order of the day. Prepare the meals immediately. Let's have turkey! Doughnuts! Kibble! You there," he said, beckoning grandly to an imaginary servant. "Go fetch the royal ball."

Tom laughed with delight. *Wait until I get home and tell everyone where I've been!* he thought. *I wonder if they'll believe me. Even if they don't, it doesn't matter, because I shall remember this day for always and always! Imagine that! I know the prince! Maybe I can have a special spot near him when he gets crowned as king!*

The young pauper spent a sizable amount of time pretending he was Prince Edward. After a while, he tired of the game and he began to worry. He wandered over to a window and stared out at the mob, listlessly wagging his tail. Where was Edward? What if someone came into the room and wanted to know why he, Tom, had the prince's clothes on? Would they rub his nose in any mischief he might make? Would they put him in prison or hang him?

Suddenly, the door opened. A courtier dressed in purple silks and a high, feathered hat came in. Tom shrank back from the window. He waited for the courtier to scold him for pretending to be someone he was not. Maybe he would be scolded for slobbering on the silk. Or maybe he would be yelled at for shedding on the floor. Would he be thrown out by the scruff of his neck? None of those things happened, and instead of looking angry, the courtier bowed.

"Your Highness, I am Lord Hertford, at your service. Your royal presence is awaited at court."

"Oh, no . . . you misunderstand. I'm . . . not—" Tom stammered.

"If you would attend, Your Highness." The courtier bowed so low that the feather on his hat practically brushed the shiny floor.

"Oh, no!" Tom cried. "You're barking up the wrong tree! I'm not the prince! You've got the wrong guy!"

"Sire," said the attendant, "the king awaits you."

The king! Tom thought. *I smell more than kibble now . . . I smell trouble!*

There was nothing to do but heel alongside Lord Hertford as he walked down a long marble hallway. They hurried past more rooms than Tom could imagine. He was starting to get weary when Lord Hertford led him into a large chamber. Inside, a great portly man lay resting in bed, surrounded by pillows. The room smelled of medicine and bland food . . . and of something about to happen!

"Your Highness," the lord said, bowing. "I bring you your son."

Tom cowered in fear, burrowing his head under his paws. So this was the dreaded King Henry VIII who everyone was so afraid of! He looked to Tom like a sick old man, with poor color and a hacking cough. His hair and beard were gray. His skin was so pale that he looked almost like a ghost.

Surely, Tom thought, gravely ill or not, this man

would know his own son. He would surely recognize an impostor when he set eyes upon one. Tom would be punished! *Maybe I should roll over and play dead,* Tom thought. *That usually works well for me in tough situations.* He hung his head in shame and tucked his tail tightly between his legs. When he finally dared to look up, he saw, to his surprise, that the king was smiling upon him.

"My son," the king said, holding out his hands. "Come closer!"

"Your son! I know I'm cute, but I'm more of a stray than best of breed," Tom said as he hesitantly edged forward. "These are real fleas you see here," he pointed out. "The real prince and I changed clothes and now he is somewhere outside and I am here. It is all a terrible mistake that can be fixed only by finding him!"

"The real prince!" The king suddenly drew himself up a little. "What are you talking about? What ails thee, my son?" The king looked deeply concerned.

"I am not the prince, but only poor Tom Canty of Offal Court!"

King Henry looked worried. "Tom Canty? Offal Court? What place is this?" The king turned to his advisors and asked, "Why does he insist that he is someone else and lives someplace else?" He looked at Lord Hertford, who shrugged his shoulders. "Has he gone mad?" the king asked. "That would be bad timing indeed! I know I am soon to die. Edward must take my place and be crowned the new king of England." The king motioned for Tom to come closer to him. "Pray, tell me, what made you go mad and say such things?"

"It is not madness, but the truth," said Tom.

The king turned toward Lord Hertford.

"Perhaps he is just a little mad," Lord Hertford started to say, but the king interrupted him.

"Don't say that! Ever! And mad or sane, he will soon be the next king of England! You tell everyone to humor him, no matter what nonsense he speaks! No one shall say this is not the king's son!"

The king looked kindly on Tom again. "Do not look so fearful, my son."

Tom hesitated and scratched at his front leg. "I'm itching to leave. May I?" he asked.

"Leave? And go where?" said the puzzled king.

"Why, go home, sire," said Tom. "To Offal Court."

"I don't understand," the king responded. "Your place is here. Everything you could want or desire is at your command. There is no need to go anywhere else."

Tom felt his heart sink as low to the ground as his tail. "Well, may I be granted leave to go into some corner and nap? All this confusion is making me bone-tired."

Lord Hertford looked astonished. "So please Your Majesty," he said. "It is for you to command, and for us to obey. If you want to rest, so be it."

"Yes," said the king. "Let him rest. Perhaps his senses will return when he rises."

Lord Hertford pulled a bell cord. A young boy wearing blue tights and a blue satin shirt appeared. He bowed deeply to Tom. "Your page," Lord Hertford said, motioning to the boy. "He will take you to your room."

"Follow me," said the page.

Tom was led away from the king's chamber. All his thoughts of being set free seemed crushed to the ground. The page took Tom to a magnificent bedroom. It was decorated in glowing blue satin. It had a bed almost as large as the room Tom shared with his family back in Offal Court. On the wall was a huge painting of the king and Edward, both seated on a great red couch. "Sleeping in a big high bed when I'm used to the floor. That's really an elevated position," Tom said.

But when Tom leaped up and began to lie down, the page stopped him.

"What now?" cried Tom. "I'm housebroken. You don't have to worry."

"You must let me dress you for bed," the page answered.

"Dress me?" Tom cried. Still, Tom was so tired that he let the page take off his fine clothes. Then the page put a silk nightgown on him. Soon Tom was tucked underneath not one but three thick satin quilts. He had never before in his life been in a bed so comfortable, snug, and warm. "Well, sleeping *is* on my top-ten list of things I like to do," Tom told himself. "Maybe I can just catch a cat nap to get my strength back. Then I'll figure out how to get out of this mess and get home, back to my old life."

"Rest," the page advised. "Perhaps you will feel more like yourself in the morning."

More like myself, thought Tom. *I wish I were. Then I'd be back at home. I'd be romping outside in the fields and playing under the bright sun. Instead, I'm kenneled in this palace!*

Tom couldn't understand it. Dreaming of being a prince had been so pleasant when he was back at home—but there in the palace, the reality was turning into a nightmare that he couldn't seem to awaken from, no matter what he did!

Uh-oh! All the boys wanted was to change places just for a bit, and now they're getting real

paws-on experience about what it's like to be some-one else. Well, I guess if you talk the talk, you have to walk the walk, too! It's just like what's happening with Joe, who's about to start switch-hitting as "the Coach." And, like poor little Tom, this is no time to be sleeping on the job!

Chapter Four

"Okay, wake up now, girls!" Mr. Barnes called to the Tigers. There were fifteen Tigers. They were all five-year-old girls who were sitting lazily on the playing field. They were decked out in their orange shorts and T-shirts and caps. White socks poked out from their sneakers. Their hair was pulled back in pigtails or ponytails to keep it out of the way. Wishbone, who had been polishing up on his napping skills, roused himself. He stood beside Joe and Mr. Barnes. He eyed the Tigers. They were only half the size of Joe, he noted. But from where he stood, half the size was still something he would have to watch out for. He eyed their knapsacks, which he bet were filled with all kinds of delicacies. Suddenly, his nose began to tingle. *Wake up and smell the cookies!* he thought, perking up.

Mr. Barnes clapped his hands to get the little girls' attention.

"All right," he said. "Now listen up, girls. I want you to meet someone who's helping us out. His name is Joe, and he's going to be running today's practice. I want you to give him your undivided attention. Okay. Now let's all please say hello to Joe."

Emily Barnes was sitting up front, which made Wishbone a little nervous. He knew from experience that Emily could get a little overenthusiastic when it came to him. *For a little girl, she's got arms of steel,* Wishbone thought. Emily was leaning up against her best friend, Tina. Both girls had identical pigtails tied with blue ribbons. Emily looked up past Joe, right to where Wishbone was sitting. "Doggie! We want the doggie!" she cooed, motioning for Wishbone to go to her.

"Yes!" called Tina. "We want the doggie!"

Wishbone preened. "What can I say?" said Wishbone. "The ladies love me! Well, girls, you can look, but don't touch!"

Joe sighed, but Mr. Barnes gave him an encouraging pat on the shoulder. He took off his official coach's hat and handed it to Joe with great ceremony. "Remember, Joe, they're just five-year-old girls."

Joe put the coach's hat on, trying to stand taller. He cleared his throat to get the girls to focus on him.

"Good afternoon, Tigers," he said in his best take-charge voice. "We've got a lot to do, so we really need to get started."

"That's right, Joe, you tell them!" Wishbone said.

Emily curled her finger at Wishbone, beckoning him. "Wish-bone!" she sang.

"Uh-oh," said Wishbone, taking his eyes off Joe. "It's Emily again."

Emily winked at him and began fishing in her knapsack. Suddenly, she drew out a cookie and waved it at Wishbone.

Wishbone was beside himself. "I knew it! I was right! She's got one of those cookies I smelled!" He hesitated. Should he risk it? "They'll eat me alive! They don't call them Tigers for nothing! Look at the teeth in those smiles!"

"T-ball is a team sport." This time Joe was speaking louder. Wishbone turned his attention back to him. "That means we all have to work together."

Wishbone tried to show his support for Joe. He cocked his head and listened extra carefully. Out of the corner of his eye, he spied Tina pointing out the cookie.

"Here, Wishbone!" Tina cooed.

Wishbone hesitated. He had a difficult choice to make. He could grab the cookie, but then the little girls would grab him! He edged forward, paw by paw, on the grass. "I've got to be very careful. . . ." he told himself.

"By the time the season starts," Joe said, "we should be running like a machine—a well-oiled machine."

Wishbone bellied closer to the cookie. "I'm still listening, Joe!" Wishbone called. He could smell the cookie. Vanilla. Intoxicating. "Just take the cookie and walk away," he instructed himself. "Act casual," he told himself. "You're listening to Joe, you're moving on the grass a little, getting some exercise. That's all."

"So remember," Joe said, "all we have to do is—"

"Now!" Wishbone said. "Ambush that cookie!" He turned from Joe and grabbed the sweet just as the girls snatched him! He swallowed it quickly, licking his mouth to get every last crumb.

"Wishbone!" Joe called. "Girls!"

"I can't help it! I'm surrounded, Joe!" Wishbone called. The girls petted and kissed him. "Easy there!" Wishbone cried. "Watch those hands! Okay, okay. You pet this rookie, I get the cookie—that's the deal! Hey, let's see that cookie! No, not the small one. That big one over there." He bit into the sweet. "Oh, delicious! Thank you! Easy, easy!" he cried. He took another mouthful. Then he saw Joe out of the corner of his eye.

Joe shook his head at Wishbone. "You're not helping things, Wishbone!" Joe called to him.

"But I will! I will! I haven't forgotten you, Joe!" Wishbone called. "Good luck, Joe!"

"Come on, team," Joe said, clapping his hands, rousing the girls to stand. "Forget Wishbone for a moment and let's play!"

"Okay, so I'm weak," Wishbone said, returning to the sidelines. "Oh, girls, if you've got any more cookies, you know where to find me!"

Wishbone, licking the last of the cookie crumbs from his mouth, sat and watched from the stands. Joe was having the Tigers practice catching the ball in the outfield. "Okay, Emily," he called. "Pretend this ball is coming at you. Try to catch it." He threw the ball and it whizzed past her. She didn't move.

"Fetch!" Wishbone yelled.

"Emily, what's wrong?" Joe asked.

"You didn't throw the ball to me!" Emily called. "You just threw it in the air!"

Joe tried not to look exasperated. "Try again," he said. He threw the ball toward Emily and this time it thudded and rolled on the ground past Tina. "Tina! Catch the ball!" Joe called. Tina was so busy staring dreamily at the clouds in the sky that she didn't notice the ball coming toward her. Joe was getting frustrated. "Next time, stop the ball!" he said impatiently.

Wishbone could feel the tension in the air. *Uh-oh,* he thought. *Joe's getting his dander up. He's getting itchy with nerves! Joe! Joe! Stay calm! Take it from me. It's always worse when you scratch!*

"Okay, girls, pay attention to the ball!" Joe shouted. "Try to catch this!"

Wishbone watched as Joe pitched a ball to a group of girls. They were intent on playing patty-cake with their field gloves. They giggled and the ball rolled right past them.

"Girls!" Joe wailed. "The ball! You have to watch the ball!"

"Don't feel bad!" Wishbone called to Joe. "Try it again. They're just warming up!"

Joe searched the team. "Okay, let's try it again! We need this outfield practice!" Joe tossed the ball and then threw it to three Tigers, who were too busy braiding one another's hair to try to catch it. Then Joe picked up another ball and hit it to a Tiger who plopped down on the field.

She began pulling petals off a daisy. "Wishbone loves me, he loves me not," she sang as she plucked off the petals. "Wishbone loves me!" she cried happily.

"What about the game?" Joe asked. "Can't you love the game?"

"Sorry, honey, that's just puppy love," Wishbone called to the Tiger. "Anyway, I'm *man's* best friend. Man—as in grown boy. Boy—as in Joe."

"Isn't there *anyone* who wants to play?" Joe cried.

"Me! Me!" Wishbone called. "Let the dog play."

A little girl with long blond pigtails and red socks, who was named Carol, was standing off by herself. When Joe looked at her, she covered her face shyly with her hands and cowered.

"Don't be afraid of Joe," Wishbone said to her. "He doesn't bite—not even when you chew up his shoes!"

"This situation is getting desperate," Joe said. He turned to Mr. Barnes. "Okay, who are the strongest players? I'll concentrate on them."

"I'm pretty strong, Joe," Wishbone said. "Remember the time when I tore up the living room carpet all by myself?"

Mr. Barnes looked at Joe with amusement. "Strongest players? This is a team, remember, Joe?" He gave Joe an encouraging pat on the shoulder. "Patience, Joe."

Joe sighed. "Okay, one more time." He picked up the ball and batted it toward center field. "Somebody get it!" Joe shouted. The ball sailed toward the group of little girls. They all squealed and ducked, covering their heads. Joe shook his head in frustration. "What's going on out there!" he called.

"Wishbone to the rescue! This game needs some mouth-to-mouth resuscitation!" Wishbone ran over and snatched up the ball in his jaw and the girls surrounded him. "Hey, catch the ball, not me!" He tried to wriggle free. "Joe! Joe! I got their attention. Now call them off!"

"Come on, team!" Joe shouted, clapping his hands. He led them over to the T-ball stand. "Okay, team," he said, trying to sound enthusiastic. "This will get you ready in no time! Let's practice hitting the ball." He set up a ball on the tee and called over Amy, a little girl with bright red hair.

"'Atta girl, Amy!" said Wishbone.

Joe handed Amy a bat. "Try to hit the ball off the tee," he said.

She swung the bat, completely missing the ball. When she started to walk away, Joe pulled her back, trying to be patient.

"Don't give up!" he urged. "You just need a little work, that's all. Straighten that arm and lower it a bit. You're doing fine. Now, try it again."

Wishbone watched Amy hunch over the bat, then swing with all her might. This time she struck Joe squarely in the hip with the bat. Joe doubled over, wincing in pain. He rubbed and rubbed his sore hip, while the little girl giggled.

Wishbone yelped in sympathy. "It's a strike! But somehow I don't think it's the kind of hit Joe wants."

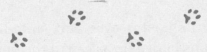

Poor Joe. Life as a coach isn't the piece of cake he thought it would be. Yup, Joe has a rude awakening ahead of him—just like the one that Mark Twain's prince and pauper are about to get.

Chapter Five

Wishbone shut his eyes and fantasized that he was Tom, curled up asleep in the prince's goose-down bed, cozy and warm. Even his fleas seemed to have taken a powder in such fine surroundings. He believed his good fortune to be but a wondrous dream. Suddenly, the sound of many footsteps started to wake him up.

Uh-oh, this is some wake-up call! I have a feeling the phrase "rise and shine" is about to take on a brand-new meaning!

The door to the royal chamber opened. Dozens of finely dressed servants entered in a grand procession. Each of them was carrying a different gleaming article of richly colored clothing. All of the attendants gathered around the bed. One courtier leaned over Tom, gently waking him more fully. "It's getting late. May it please Your Majesty to open your eyes."

Tom's eyes flew open. This was no dream! He was still in the palace! And dozens of people were standing over him. "Hello? Can I help you with anything?" he asked in his most polite voice.

"Commence the dressing!" proclaimed the man nearest Tom.

"Dressing? What am I, a salad?"

"Yes, Lord Hertford," said one of the servants.

"Lord who?" said Tom, still half asleep. "Commence what?" Hands reached out to help Tom up. "Hey! Hey!" he called. "Wait a minute! You—Lord Hertford, that's thy name, wait, wait, I can put on my own clothes! Keep your hands to yourself, please! Hey! Hey! My coat's not reversible! Leave me alone!"

"Would it please Your Highness to remain still while the dressing proceeds!" said Lord Hertford.

"Hey, your hands are cold," Tom complained. "And I told you, I'm *not* the prince!"

The courtiers exchanged glances. "The king commands it. We must humor this madness," one whispered to another.

"Wait a minute! I heard that!" Tom said snappishly. "And I'm not crazy, and I'm not the prince of Wales. I'm Tom Canty of Offal Court, not Tom Canty of the palace."

The servants paid no attention to his protest. Instead, they formed a long line around him. One by one, the royal garments were taken up and passed solemnly from one man to another to another and another and yet another. A shirt and pants and vest and coat, all covered with jewels, were handed down from one man to the next. It was just like a bucket of water being passed down the line at a fire. The clothing made its long and tedious journey, beginning with the first lord of the buckhounds. He, in turn, passed it to the second gentleman of the bedchamber, who then handed it to the master of the wardrobe. The master then passed it to the chief steward of the household until it finally came to Tom. Each garment had to go through this slow process. By the time an article of clothing came close to Tom, he tried to get in a quick chew, or start up a friendly game of tug-of-war just to liven things up, but each time he failed. When the servants finally came to his stockings, Tom felt himself so wearily grateful that he was about to thank all of them. The first lord of the bedchamber was about to pull stockings on Tom when he suddenly gasped. "See here, my lord!" the lord called to the archbishop, pointing something out in the stockings.

"What? What?" Tom asked.

The archbishop turned pale. "See this, my lord!" he cried to yet another lord.

"What's wrong?" Tom asked. "Can't you tell me? Wait, I've got an idea. Would it be so terrible if I went without socks today? What if we do something different? If you want to make yourself useful, how about a tummy rub?"

"A run!" one of the lords cried. "We can't put these stockings on you. We must fetch a new pair."

Tom shook his head, astonished. He watched the socks traveling slowly back to the door of the bedchamber, passed by one set of hands to another. "Wait,

I've got another great idea!" he cried. "Why don't you let *me* fetch the fresh socks? Fetching is one of my greatest skills, you know. I'm a real champion."

"Now, now," soothed one of the lords, patting Tom's shoulder. "It won't be long."

But getting the new socks seemed to take forever. "No socks!" Tom cried. To his surprise, everyone listened. Tom was finally dressed, but he was so dog-tired that all he wanted to do was fall back to sleep again.

"The dressing has finished!" Lord Hertford proclaimed.

Tom sat up and watched gratefully as the procession left. "Wait a minute!" he said. "Can't you stay awhile and play? A quick game of hide-the-crown, maybe? Or what about a game of 'open the front gate and let the pauper escape?'"

"Games are not the order of the day, Your Highness," Lord Hertford said with no humor in his voice. "Now you must take care of business."

"Business? What business?"

"Follow me, sire," Lord Hertford said. He led Tom to another large room.

Along the way, they passed a guard dragging a ragged man into a room and then slamming the door. "I didn't do it!" the terrified man cried.

"*What* didn't he do?" Tom whispered.

Lord Hertford shook his head. "Most likely he stole something. But Your Highness doesn't have to worry. We catch and punish all in the kingdom who do something wrong."

"You do?" Tom asked, trying to steady his voice. Tom felt his four paws freeze into place. Punishment! He was the one who would be punished most severely! The members of the royal household would be very angry when they found out Tom was sleeping in the soft bed reserved for Edward. They would surely be furious when they saw he was getting all the respect and honor meant for Edward. *But it's not my fault!* Tom thought with a sense of panic. Hadn't he tried and tried to tell everyone at the palace that he was not the prince? Was it his fault that nobody believed him? The more he insisted he was not the prince, the more the attendants ignored him. They treated him as if he were crazy. "If I'm to survive here, I had better act like a prince until I can go back to being myself," Tom said. "I had better keep my eyes and ears open and my nose to the ground until I figure out what to do. No one is going to tell me or show me."

Tom was brooding over his situation when Lord Hertford led him down a great hall and into yet another room, with windows running along both sides of the walls. Tom was instructed to sit at a long oak table. In front of him was a purple quill pen, a bottle of ink, and a stack of papers so high that it practically tickled Tom's nose.

"Business as usual," said Lord Hertford.

But this royal life was all new to Tom. Nothing seemed usual to him there in the palace. He sat up and waited and tried to look as if he knew what he was doing and as if nothing could possibly surprise him.

Presently, six courtiers came into the room and approached Tom. They bowed and acted as if he were the real prince. Lord Hertford picked up the pile of papers in front of Tom and read what was on them. Some were petitions, formal requests, for more money to build roads or houses. Some were proclamations to make a certain man a duke, or another man an earl, or some people *both* a duke and an earl. *What should I decide?* Tom kept asking himself silently. Every time he had to make a decision, he glanced over at Lord Hertford, looking for clues. "I should sign this," Tom said, and when the lord looked relaxed, he went ahead and signed it. When the lord frowned, however, Tom suddenly said, "I changed my mind," and he didn't sign at all. *He doesn't even realize he's helping me!* Tom thought. *It's lucky for me that he has such a readable face!*

After a while, Tom tried to figure out what else he might do as prince.

"I wonder if I could make my mother duchess of Offal Court!" Tom said. "She'd surely love that! Or maybe I could give myself the Royal Order of Bone Master! Or declare myself Exalted Emperor of Fetch! I could even establish a Dig Zone."

Lord Hertford laughed. "What a sense of humor!" he said. He presented Tom with the next petition. It was a request for more tax money so an earl could build a home.

The work was not finished until what seemed like hours had passed. The whole time Tom kept hoping for the prince's return. Finally, Lord Hertford took Tom back to his room, six servants following behind them. What had at first appeared so grand now seemed more like a prison than a palace.

"I'll return before dinner time," Lord Hertford informed Tom.

"Dinner!" Tom felt his spirits lift a little, for he had begun to get a bit hungry. But he felt happier only for a short time. When he looked around the room, it seemed suddenly larger and lonelier than any room he had ever been in before. "What am I going to do all day? Who am I going to do it with? I'm lonely!"

Lord Hertford smiled, but didn't answer. When he left the room, he shut the door.

Tom went over to the window and looked longingly out toward the street. "Oh, Prince, where are you? I don't think I belong in your clothes. What have I done that I should be taken away from the fresh air and the fields and be shut up here so? I want to be outside in London." He shook himself, leaving a pile of fur on the floor. "Why can't shedding this role be as easy as shedding all this fur?"

Palace-schmalace! A dog's *home* is his castle— and that's just where Tom wants to be! But hang on, because it looks as if Edward is going to get the jump on Tom by showing up at Tom's house—and I'm just the pup to imagine myself in the role!

Chapter Six

The little prince made his way through the streets of London. Everything looked strange to him. The dirt and the crowds were unfamiliar and scary. The streets were so crooked and narrow that he could hardly walk without bumping into someone. Every time he did, the person he had knocked into pushed him roughly. Edward tumbled to the ground. Soon, his poor paws were cut and bleeding, and his coat was so matted that he despaired of ever getting a grooming brush through it. He was tired and hungry and caked with grime. He sat for a moment in an alleyway. He was soon deep in a fitful sleep.

The next morning, when he woke up, the poor young prince was starving. He stretched all four of his paws and tried to feel hopeful. The air was thick with smells he didn't recognize. Most of them weren't pleasant. "I smell dirt and sickness and sour milk!" Edward said, then took another deep sniff. "It all makes me long for the royal bath!" He covered his nose with his paw for a moment. "This doesn't help!" he said. "The thing to do is try to find the pauper's family," the prince told himself. "I'll explain to them what has happened. I shall clear this mess up straightaway. They'll return me to the palace, and then their own son can be returned to them. Then everyone will be happy and back in his rightful place." He tried to remember the name of the place where the pauper had told him he lived. "Awful Cute," he mused. "No, that's not it!" He wracked his brain. "Okra Carrot—" he suggested. "No." Then, like a candle suddenly lighted, the name came to him in a blaze of memory. "Offal Court!" the prince exclaimed. "That's it! Offal Court! That shouldn't be hard to find!"

He began to feel a bit more hopeful. That put a slight spring in his step and gave a new lift to his tail. He began to notice, too, that there was a new smell in the air, a pleasurable tang. Food! It must be food! *Oh, what an interesting scent. I do believe I'm hungry,* he thought. *This could be a great opportunity for me to sample the local cuisine! I bet the citizens have all manner of delicious things—chicken à la Offal Village, perhaps, or maybe a whole plateful of lamb à la Tom.*

Edward started to try to find the source of that rich and wondrous odor. Suddenly, a hand grabbed him by the scruff of his neck! He twisted around to see the most frightening-looking and dirty man he had ever encountered. He had long raggedly cut black hair and a black beard. His eyes were so dark that it was impossible to tell what he was thinking, except that it didn't seem very nice. His clothing was all muddy-colored and torn and held together with bits of string. Both of his shoes had gaping holes in them. Edward thought of turning tail and running. Then he reminded himself that he was the prince of Wales! He had no reason to be afraid of anyone. *These are my people. Be brave!* he thought.

"You're out in the streets and you haven't brought me any money!" the man shouted at Edward in a great booming voice.

"What are you talking about?" asked Edward.

"If I don't break all your bones, then I'm not John Canty!"

The prince suddenly relaxed. "You're the pauper's father! What great fortune! I am Edward, the prince of Wales. Thank goodness, I found you. Now I don't have to keep looking for Offal Court." He drew himself up. "I order thee to take me to the palace immediately. I'm hungry and I'd like food."

John Canty roared with laughter. "You'd like food, you say! Why, you've gone stark-ravin' mad!" He grabbed the prince up.

"Hey! Unhand me! I'm the prince of Wales!" The young prince struggled with all his might, but he was no match for John Canty.

"Hungry for food, are ye? Well, I'll give you food for thought. You'll beg or be beaten!" Canty threatened him. "And you'll starve!"

"Starve! As long as there are food bowls, princes don't starve!" Edward insisted. But all he had to do was

look at the fierce and determined glare in John Canty's angry eyes to begin to get worried. "Do they?" he asked meekly.

No, indeed, princes don't starve! But nobody believes that Edward is the prince. They think Tom is! And as prince, Tom is the one about to have his belly filled with all manner of wonderful taste treats. As for me, I'm starting to imagine myself as Tom again, and I can see the palace so clearly that I can practically taste the excitement—*and* all of the food.

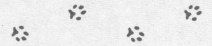

Tom couldn't believe his eyes. He was in an enormous yellow room with nothing in it but a huge, long marble table. Although the table had forty chairs around it, he was the only one seated, right at the very head. The table was covered with a lavish blue silk tablecloth. Twenty-five attendants in blue silk hats stood around the table. They kept their hands folded in front of them and watched him expectantly.

"The prince is about to eat!" they buzzed to one another. Six servants appeared out of a room Tom guessed must be the kitchen, carrying steaming golden platters of turkey, beef, and fish, and long golden trays piled high with scrumptious-looking fruits and breads.

Poor Tom had only dreamed about food like this. The attendants set the platters down and bowed to him with a rustling of silk and satin.

At once Tom's mood began to improve. Maybe life at the palace wouldn't be so terrible if there were meals like this to look forward to. "I should be fine acting like the prince here. One thing I know is how to eat food!" Tom said. "At least I think I do!" But then he looked around, and even though the room was filled with people, he was the only one with a place setting laid out in front of him. How was he supposed to know how they ate around here if there was no one to watch and study?

Tom hesitated. He'd have to pretend he knew what he was doing. He nosed out a huge platter of turkey, big enough to feed his family for a month.

"Uh, anyone got a doggie bag for this?" he inquired pleasantly. "I mean, I might be hungry later, right? No need to let all this food go to waste." He stared at a huge turkey leg set before him.

Tom's eyes were as big as his stomach. He didn't know what to try first.

"The food here is said to be superb! Four-star, in fact! Is there a menu to choose from? What's the catch of the day? And what's for dessert? Oh, look over there! Wow! What a bone!"

A young boy approached and picked up the turkey leg.

"Hey, that's mine!" Tom cried.

A servant stopped Tom from grabbing the turkey leg. "Let the food taster do his job, sire."

Food taster! Tom had never heard of such a person, but he thought he had better keep quiet about it. But why did the boy have to taste the food?

The boy bent forward and sniffed at the turkey leg before Tom. "It doesn't smell poisoned, sire," the boy said to Tom.

Poisoned! Tom flinched and sat back. There was more to being a prince than met the eye, even to eyes as keen as Tom's. A prince had enemies! He never thought of that before! It didn't seem fair that the food taster should get sick—or worse—on his account.

He motioned to the food taster. "Don't eat that!" he advised, but the boy took a big bite out of the turkey leg. Everyone seemed to hold their breath, especially the boy, who swallowed hard and then waited.

"Well?" Lord Hertford asked finally.

The food taster broke into a big grin. "Delicious!" he declared.

"Wait a minute! I could have told you it was delicious if you had let me!" Tom said indignantly. "I can tell it's delicious just by smelling it."

"No ill effects," Lord Hertford proclaimed. "The boy is still healthy and alive."

"You can eat without worry, Your Highness," the boy said, and everyone sighed in relief.

Tom wrapped his paws around the hefty leg and put to his mouth. "Well, I'm glad you're okay, but you sure did take a pretty big bite," he said. He looked down the table. "It's okay. Nothing else looks suspicious. I can take it from here, thank you kindly. Food tasting is my calling. I'd be more than happy to take a taste of everything twice—or three times, if you think that's better. I probably should just finish everything, to be on the safe side."

A dish of water was set before him, with a few rose petals floating in it. *What's this?* Tom thought. *It must be soup,* he decided, then bent and lapped from the bowl. "This is weak soup!" he proclaimed. He didn't want to appear rude, so he licked his chops in appreciation. "Even though it's quite tasty, you wouldn't happen to have any salt, would you? A bit of pepper? Maybe some salami to slice into it?"

Gently, Lord Hertford lifted Tom's paws and washed them clean in the water. "You must be tired, sire. You're drinking from the finger bowl that's meant for washing your hands."

"Oh, I knew that," said Tom. "Yes, yes, I'm very tired."

"Is everything all right?" Lord Hertford inquired.

Tom nodded. "Guess my manners aren't exactly up to scratch today, are they?"

Tom ran his tongue across his mouth to clean it, stopping in mid-lick when he saw a servant staring at him. He searched the table. In front of him was a fine piece of pure white cloth. The servant stared at the cloth. Hesitantly, Tom picked it up in his paws. When he saw the servant relax, he touched the cloth to his mouth. The servant sighed in relief. *My goodness!* Tom thought. *How will I ever get used to the customs here?*

Just then, another lord arrived and bowed before

the company. "My fellow Englishmen," he announced, "I come bearing sad news. King Henry is dead."

Oh, no, thought Tom. *The prince's father! He was really kind to me. I bet the prince is going to feel really sad.* He bowed his head and gave a respectful whimper, but then he felt all eyes glued upon him. When he looked up, no one else looked unhappy. In fact, they were all nodding and smiling at him.

"What?" said Tom, starting to feel uneasy. "What's going on here? Did I miss a punch line? Tell me, because I love a good joke as much as the next guy."

One of the courtiers lifted up his hands. "Let the joy ring out! In three days the young prince will be crowned king!"

Tom sat up straight. His fur stood on end. "What? You can't crown me king! Three days' time is Thursday! I'll be trapped here forever! Oh, no, the coronation! I'm not going to just get to see it—I'm going to *be* it! Suddenly I've lost my appetite! Edward, please come home! Come home now!!!!"

Uh-oh, the plot is thickening, as we say in the literary biz. The fur is really about to fly now that John Canty's got the prince collared, and the pauper is on a tight leash at court—and wait—wait! I think I smell even more trouble, because Joe is about to coach the big game!

Chapter Seven

*A*h, *breakfast, the most important meal of the day,* Wishbone thought as he gobbled his down. *Besides lunch, that is. And let's not forget dinner. And, of course, snacks—we can't forget snacks.* He licked his bowl clean and eyed the french toast Joe and Ellen were finishing at the kitchen table. Joe pulled off an end piece of his toast and gave it to Wishbone.

"'Atta boy, Joe," Wishbone said. "It's better to give than to receive! And, in my case, I was born to be on the receiving end!"

"So," Ellen said to Joe, "today's the big game. Are you excited?"

Joe speared the last piece of toast. "I'll be excited when it's over. I'm never coaching again."

"Oh, Joe, it can't be that bad," Ellen said, pouring Joe some more orange juice. "They're only five-year-old girls."

Wishbone turned to Ellen. "They're barracudas, Ellen. Don't let them fool you."

"It's tough, Mom," Joe said. "I hate to admit it, but without Mr. Barnes, I'd never make it through this game."

Ellen ruffled his hair. "You'll be fine."

The doorbell rang. "Is that the mailman?" Wishbone asked hopefully. "Nice guy. Ever since he gave me those free samples of dog treats, he's got *my* stamp of approval!"

"I'll get it," Joe said.

He got up from his seat and opened the door. There was Mrs. Barnes standing on the back porch. Beside her were Emily and Tina, dressed in their yellow Tigers outfits.

"Mrs. Barnes!" Joe said.

"Uh-oh, and she's got two of the barracudas with her!" Wishbone said.

Mrs. Barnes looked harried. "Joe, I'm so happy you're still here. There's been a big change of plans. Mr. Barnes is home packing. I have to rush him to the airport."

"But we have a big game today," Joe said.

Mrs. Barnes shook her head. "Sorry, honey, but it's a last-minute business trip. Mr. Barnes has to go right away, and he needs you to run the game. He's counting on you, in fact."

Joe looked shocked. "He wants me to run the game all by myself?"

Mrs. Barnes nodded. "You can do it. You'll be great. And I need to leave Emily and Tina here with you." She gently pushed the girls forward. "Girls, be good."

"We will," they sang. The girls looked at each other. They giggled in a way that made Wishbone very, very nervous.

"Do they know the meaning of the word 'good'?" Wishbone wondered. "Should we get them a dictionary? What do you think, Joe? Maybe if they have the words right in front of them . . ."

"Thanks, Joe. I have to rush," said Mrs. Barnes. "I'll see you later at the game. Now have fun." She turned and left.

Astonished, Joe looked at his mother. "Fun?" he echoed. "I'm supposed to have fun?"

Wishbone contemplated his food dish. "Fun. This situation calls for a bigger breakfast," he decided. "Ellen! Oh, Ellen! Any refills available?"

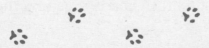

Joe, Ellen, and the girls played checkers in the living room until it was time to go to the game. All Wishbone had to do was look at the way Joe was tapping his foot on the floor to know he was so anxious about the T-ball game that he couldn't concentrate at all. "Calm down, Joe," Wishbone said, rubbing against Joe's leg. "Here, try a natural hands-on remedy for nerves—dog fur!"

"King me!" Emily sang, bringing her piece to the finish line.

"Great! I'm losing at checkers!" Joe moaned.

Emily smiled and ruffled Joe's hair. "It's not whether you win or lose, it's how you play the game. You know that."

"Tell that to Mr. Barnes," Joe said. "He's counting on me!"

"And you'll be terrific," Ellen said. She stood up. "Okay, gang, let's hit the road."

"Dogs in the front seat, barracudas in back!" Wishbone said.

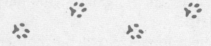

That afternoon, the weather was perfect for the big game. The stands were full of parents and friends, some of them already snacking on picnic lunches. The Tigers and the Banshees teams were on the field. They gathered around their coaches, getting their pre-game pep talk.

Wishbone sat in the stands, waiting for Joe to call him down onto the field. He had a dog's-eye view of the action two rows ahead of Ellen and Wanda Gilmore, her friend, neighbor, and owner of one of Wishbone's favorite yards! It certainly wasn't as rewarding as being right in the thick of things. He watched Joe draw himself up in his most coach-like manner.

"All right, Tigers," Joe said. "From what I hear, the Banshees are pretty tough this year. But if you just put your minds to it—"

One little girl interrupted. "Where's Wishbone?"

"Oh, my fan club! My ladies-in-waiting!" Wishbone called. "Not too close, girls!"

"Wishbone's going to watch the game from the stands today," Joe said.

"I have to stay in the stands?" Wishbone said, surprised. "Wait a minute, Joe, the *stands?* Shouldn't we talk about this before any final decision is made? Isn't there an umpire we can call in to make the final decision?"

"But we want him now!" cried Emily.

"You girls needs to concentrate now," Joe pointed out. "You can see him after the game."

Wishbone settled back glumly into the stands. "Exiled again! Forced to be a cheerleader. Well, that's what you get for being too cute. Right, Ellen?"

He turned to look at her. Ellen was breathing in the spring air.

"This is a perfect day for a season opener," Wanda proclaimed.

Ellen nodded in agreement. "Nice blue sky, balmy spring breeze."

She leaned back, stretching, when suddenly, from behind her, a voice boomed in her ear. "Come on, Tigers! Clobber those Banshees!"

Wishbone cocked his head. He recognized the big burly man in the loud shirt who was *still* shouting.

"Oh, look, it's Mr. King," Wishbone said. "And he's exercising his vocal cords!"

Ellen twisted around to look at Mr. King with annoyance. Then she looked back at Wanda and rolled her eyes in exasperation. "So much for peace and quiet," Ellen said.

"So how long is the game?" Wanda asked.

Ellen rolled her eyes. "One hour. One long hour."

"Come on, Katie, make Daddy proud!" Mr. King shouted, so loudly that Wishbone was startled.

"There's one in every game," Ellen said with a sigh.

Just then a loud whistle blew. "The game's starting!" Wishbone said with glee. "And I, for one, am primed for action!" He sat up higher on his hind legs. "Oh, look, there's Sam and David! And Mrs. Barnes! Yoo-hoo! Over here!" Wishbone barked and scooted over to make room for his close friends.

"Hi, Wishbone," said Sam, climbing up and patting him. David sat down beside her.

Mrs. Barnes climbed up to sit by Ellen. "I made it just in time!" she said.

Chapter Eight

Just in time, indeed! The Tigers pulled themselves into their starting lineup at bat, and the Banshees spread out across the outfield. The woman sitting in front of Wishbone stood up. Wishbone balanced on his hind legs, trying to see over her. "Uh . . . ma'am . . . ma'am!" he called politely. "I'm a watchdog and I need to *watch!* Could you sit down, please?" He barked encouragingly and the woman turned around to face him.

"What a cutie pie!" she said, petting Wishbone, then sitting back down.

"Beauty does have its rewards," agreed Wishbone, who now had a clear view of the playing field. "And now, on to the game! Go, Tigers!" Wishbone yapped.

Tina was up at bat first. She leaned over the ball and then hit it with a resounding *thwack!*

"Come on, Tina!" Joe shouted. "Run! Run!"

"'Atta girl, Tina!" Wishbone shouted.

Tina took off as the Banshees scrambled for the

ball. She sprinted to first base, and went on to second, but then something strange happened. Instead of going on to third base, she kept running, as far as her legs would take her, straight into the outfield!

"Tina!" Joe shouted. "No! This way! Come back! Come back!"

Wishbone, watching in the stands, hid his face in his paws.

Joe shook his head, completely discouraged. "Next up at bat," he said.

Wishbone leaned forward, trying to see who was next. It was Amy's turn. She picked up the bat, leaned forward, swung, and missed. Amy's lower lip started to tremble and she burst into tears.

"Oh, no! I can't stand the sight of tears!" Wishbone said.

"Come on, you're doing fine," Joe said to Amy. "Give it one more try."

"Mom!" she cried. "I want my mom!"

"Would a cute little dog do instead?" Wishbone offered.

"Oh, don't cry!" Joe said, exasperated. From the stands, the girl's mother suddenly appeared and gave Joe a disgusted look.

"Saved by the mom!" Wishbone said.

"You call yourself a coach!" Amy's mother accused Joe. "What do you think you're doing making my little girl cry?"

"I didn't make her cry!" Joe said.

"That's right, ma'am," Wishbone added. "If you

look closely, I think you'll agree she's crying all on her own."

"I'm trying to help her!" Joe said insistently.

"Some help! And some coach you are!" the woman said. She led her daughter off the field. "Come on, honey, we're going home," she said.

"Wait! We need her!" Joe pleaded.

"And Joe needs me for moral support!" Wishbone said, starting down the stands.

Suddenly Ellen caught sight of him. "No, no, Wishbone, stay here," Ellen said.

"Benched again!" Wishbone said, settling back down. Wishbone watched the game through the first inning, and the second, and finally the third. From his position, he could see how badly the game was going. The scoreboard read 10–5, in favor of the Banshees! A Tiger was running to a base, and it looked as if she was going to keep right on running past the base!

"Hold it! Hold it!" Joe called. He stood in front of the base, catching the girl in his arms before she could run past him. The two of them nearly tumbled to the ground.

"Boy, she almost knocked the wind right out of Joe's sails!" Wishbone said.

Another little Tiger was running to second base when she suddenly stopped, crouched, and leisurely took off her sneaker to remove a stone from inside it.

"What are you doing?" Joe cried. "Forget your shoe! Get up! Run! Run!" The Tiger began to tie her sneaker back on, just as a Banshee tagged her out.

"Oh, no!" shouted Mr. King, covering his face with his hands.

"Somebody help me!" Joe pleaded.

He studied the lineup. Carol, the shy girl, was next, but she was being pushed by the other Tigers farther and farther to the back of the batting line.

"I can bat!" Carol exclaimed. "Let me at least try! Come on, give me a chance!"

"You're no batter!" one of the girls said.

"I'll help you, Carol!" Wishbone said. "I'll run diversion and you grab the bat!" Wishbone again started to climb down the stands.

"Stay, Wishbone!" Ellen called.

"Give me a chance!" Carol repeated.

"I know just how you feel," Joe said to Carol.

"So do I," Wishbone added. "You've been cut down before you can show them what you've got!"

"Hey, stop that!" Joe called to the girls who were pushing Carol, but they ignored him, shoving her right to the end of the line. "Come on, girls, give her a chance!"

Joe suddenly beckoned to Carol, who touched her

chest in surprise. "Me? You want me?" She walked over to Joe.

"I want you to bat next," Joe told her. "You can do it. I'll help you." He moved to the front of the line with her. "Carol's up next," Joe told the team.

"There goes the game," a Tiger grumbled.

Wishbone barked at the Tiger. "If you want to pet me, you have to be nice," he said.

Wishbone angled himself so he could watch Carol batting. Carol took a swing and missed.

"Here, stand closer to the ball," Joe instructed.

Carol took a step forward. She swung again and missed again.

"That was better," Joe said. "Now swing a little harder."

Carol sighed. She swung harder and missed! She looked as if she were going to cry.

"That's all right. You're getting better," Joe said. "Just remember, stand closer to the ball. Swing harder next time."

It was time for the teams to change places.

"Banshees' turn at bat!" Joe called. The Tigers scattered in the field, and the Banshees lined up to bat.

"Excuse me, but does anybody need an extra second-base dog?" Wishbone barked. "Because I know just the pup to pep up this game!"

A Banshee with long black braids swung and hit the ball out to left field.

"Get it!" Joe urged. The ball spun past three Tigers, who were standing around and braiding one another's hair. "Come on, girls, we're right in the middle of the game!" Joe pleaded.

Joe's in trouble, Wishbone thought, pacing back and forth in the stands, *and he's about to be in even bigger trouble, judging from the look on Mr. King's face. He's going right toward Joe!*

Mr. King lumbered down from the stands and walked out on the field. He tapped Joe on the shoulder. "We're in the last inning here. The score is six to thirteen, in favor of the Banshees. What's your strategy?"

"My strategy?" Joe said, puzzled.

"Uh-oh," Wishbone said. "Do we have a strategy, Joe?"

"Yes. I'm a concerned parent, and I don't like what I see here. I don't like it at all." He looked across the field and boomed out to the players, "Come on, Tigers, we can still win the war!"

Joe tugged on his coach's hat. "Sir, I'm doing my best. Coaching is harder than it looks."

"Don't tell me about dealing with kids. I'm a parent, young man. I know all about it. Besides, my daughter is out there," said Mr. King, putting his hands firmly on his hips.

In the stands, Wanda heard the commotion. "What's going on out there?" she asked Ellen. "Mr. King shouldn't be out on the field like that."

Ellen squinted out at the field. "I don't know, but I don't like the looks of it."

"Neither do I," Wishbone said. "Joe needs me, I can tell."

"Come on, Katie, show them how it's done!" Mr. King shouted. He turned to Joe. "For starters, we can change the lineup. The way you have it is crazy."

There was a resounding *crack!* Wishbone perked up his ears. A Banshee had hit a ball and it was sailing across the field to some waiting Tigers! It flew past Emily, who was sitting down yawning. It rippled past Amy, who was cartwheeling. It zoomed past Tina, twirling around in circles. Finally, it rolled past Carol, who was playing a game of catch with her own mitt.

Wishbone hid his face with his paws. *Oh, no, this is a disaster!* he thought.

Mr. King pursed his lips. "Well, there goes the season," he said.

Joe threw his hands up in frustration. "Why is this happening to me?"

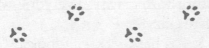

Joe, your life as coach has hit rock bottom. But don't worry, you can still get out of this if you just stand tall. Sometimes all you need is the right kind of help to get back into the winner's circle! Like the kind of help the prince and the pauper are going to need in our story!

Chapter Nine

*I*f *I can see it, I can be it!* Wishbone thought. And see it, he could! He fantasized that he was the prince of Wales. He was dressed in rags, and his fur was matted. He was sitting at the rough wood table in the pauper's dimly lit dwelling. Trying to get the pauper's family to believe his story wasn't easy. Everyone was acting as though he were crazy!

"I am Edward, prince of Wales!" the prince yelped. "Why don't you believe me and help me? I need to get back to my rightful home."

The pauper's mother started to weep. She leaned along the splintered wood table and ran her hands through her wild gray hair. She drew her torn shawl around her ragged dress. The dress was so faded that Edward could hardly tell what its original color was. "Oh, Tom, poor lad! What could possibly make thee say such things?"

"He's a regular crazy one, he is," John Canty declared.

The pauper's mother reached over and petted the boy she thought was her son.

"A little behind the ears," Edward said. He looked around the house, which was much too small for one person, let alone three people. The walls were chipped and bare, the floor covered with dirt and dust. A cracked black pot was in the fireplace. The room smelled of stale bread and too much grime and hunger.

"Oh, my poor child. Shake off this gruesome dream. Look upon me and know thy mother, who loves thee!"

The prince drew himself up. He looked around at the pauper's poor dwelling. He was itchy to leave, and itchy about his fur, too. When he looked down, he saw that he now had many fleas! "It appears that Tom and I have swapped more than clothing!" he said, scratching.

"Oh, my son!" cried the mother. "Tell me thee knows me!"

"I'm sorry, but I have never seen you before!"

The pauper's mother turned to John Canty. "Sir, he is so tired. Tomorrow he'll be himself again. Do not force him to go out and beg today."

John Canty laughed. "Beg? I would not force such a thing. This lad will *steal* for his supper." He grabbed the prince up by the scruff of his neck. "Come on. I'll keep a nice tight leash on thee."

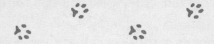

Outside, crowds had gathered and there was great rejoicing. All the people might be wearing ragged clothing, but the women had arranged flowers in their hair. The men had polished their old boots. Everyone's face was bright with excitement and color. There was a line of bonfires stretching out as far as the eye could see.

What's going on? the prince wondered silently. He didn't dare ask John Canty, who was striding deep into the streets. Canty dragged the prince so roughly behind him that he scraped the skin from Edward's very paws.

"Well, Your Highness," John Canty said to the prince, "we expect a high profit today, what with all these rich and unsuspecting folks about. Follow those people over there and see what ye can get from them." He sniffed at the air. "I smell money!" he cried with glee.

"Well, I smell trouble—big trouble!" said Edward. "And maybe some kibble, too." He shook himself away from John Canty. "I'll not beg or steal," proclaimed the prince.

"Oh, you won't, won't you! Why, then—" said John Canty, growing more and more angry. He lifted up his hand, as if he were about to strike the prince.

Edward shrank back in fear, and he covered his head with his paws.

Just then a reveler stopped them. He thrust a gold, two-handled cup filled with bubbling ale toward John Canty. "Won't you drink from a loving cup in celebration?" he shouted.

Let me just interrupt our story for an important literary message. A *loving cup* was a large, two-handled mug used in the sixteenth century. The reason for the two handles? So the drinker's hands would be too occupied to kill anyone—which back in those days was something to worry about! Okay, that's it. Now, back to our tale—because my tail is wagging in anticipation of what happens next!

John Canty tried to push past the reveler, ignoring the loving cup thrust before him. "Take away thy hand and let me pass. I have work to do."

"Work! This is no time to work. This is a time of celebration." The reveler raised the loving cup high into the air. "Nay, thou shalt not pass until the citizens drink to the coronation of King Edward this very Thursday!"

"Coronation! That's a different story! Give me that cup." John Canty lifted the cup up to his lips with both hands and threw his head back to drink.

"Coronation!" echoed the prince, his ears perking straight up. He was suddenly horrified. "My father's dead?" He began to cry, wiping the tears away with his paws. "And who's getting crowned? Is everyone in the city feasting in celebration of the pauper and not me? I'm to be the next king of England, not Tom! I've got to get back to the palace and regain my old life before it's too late!"

He looked around for some way to escape. The pauper's father was busy drinking, the reveler clapping him on the back. Edward saw his chance. He suddenly sprinted off on all fours as fast as he could run. By the time John Canty looked up again, the prince was halfway down the road.

"Come back, fool!" John Canty cried. He started to run after the prince, raising one mighty fist.

Edward ran so fast that the very fleas fell from his fur. He kept running and running until he was soon lost in the crowd. He made his way through the busy, dirty streets, right up until he got to the palace. There was a great celebration in progress, with mobs of people watching and participating. There was wild dancing. Nobles were decked out in long robes dusted with gold. It was all a great pleasure to behold for everyone but the ragged little prince of Wales. Edward fought for admission through the gates and into the palace courtyard. He pushed his way toward the gates, waving his tail like a banner. Exhausted, he finally reached the gates. Then he took the bars in his teeth and shook them for entrance.

"I am the prince of Wales!" he cried. "Gain me entrance! As forlorn and friendless as I be, yet will I not be driven from my ground, but will maintain it!"

The mob laughed at him. One among the crowd cried, "The prince! He says he's the prince of Wales! And I'm the king of Spain! Let's crown him in mud!" They all taunted and mocked him. Soon, they began to shove him and kick him and tear at his clothing and his fur. Finally, they hurled him into the mud. The poor little prince was terrified.

Just then a hand grabbed at him and lifted him upright.

"Thank you, whoever you are!" Edward said gratefully. Then he looked up into a most kindly face.

"Come with me, for ye shall find no lesser friend or protector than Miles Hendon here," the man said. "I am at your service."

Never had young Edward seen such a sight. The man was not quite as dirty as the rest of the mob, but he was not exactly clean, either. His clothing was not the same rags and tatters of the crowd, but it was torn in places and terribly faded. At his side, the man wore a long sword that was rusted in several places. Although he had a bright blue plume stuck in his hat, it was broken and missing many pieces. It could hardly be called a proper plume at all.

"Oh, look, another prince in disguise!" a man in the crowd said mockingly about Miles.

Miles ignored him. Instead, he held out his hand

for the prince to grasp. "I don't care who you say ye be. Mad or not mad, thou be a brave and gallant lad for standing thy ground, and for that I will lead you to safety," Miles promised. "Have no fear. You will come along with me."

The prince desperately wanted to gain admittance back into his palace, but he knew he might be torn apart by the crowd if he tried it again. "I'll come back later," he told himself. "Maybe later they will believe me. The thing to do now is to be safe." So, grateful, the prince grabbed hold of Miles's trousers leg in his mouth. "Sorry, I didn't mean to slobber," Edward said.

Miles guided him expertly through the teeming city. They wound in and out of the crowds, and across London Bridge itself.

Suddenly, a great cry rang out among the mob. "The king is dead! Long live the king!"

My father is dead! Edward thought. He started to cry again. *My father is dead, and I am now king!*

"Don't cry. We will soon be there," Miles said.

Edward followed Miles Hendon down the dirty streets and alleyways. Edward became more and more exhausted, and more and more cold. Finally, they reached a small inn where Miles lodged.

"Home-sweet-home!" Miles said. He opened the door and led Edward up three steep flights of rickety wooden stairs. By the time they got to the top, the prince could barely move one paw after the other anymore. Miles's dwelling was a most humble apartment, with only a wobbly table, a threadbare rug, and a lumpy-looking bed. The walls were bare. The windows were broken and patched with bits of paper, but even so, the wind whistled through.

"Gee, and I was worried he was going to ask if I was housebroken, but I'd hardly call this a house, and everything in it *already* looks broken," Edward said.

The prince looked around. After spotting the one small bed pushed in the corner, he immediately stumbled toward it and fell onto it.

"Call me when food is served," the prince murmured. Then he quickly fell asleep.

When the prince awoke, it was Tuesday, one day closer to the coronation. He discovered to his surprise that he was warm and cozy in Miles's bed. His new friend's ragged jacket was blanketed snugly about him. Miles was sleeping on the floor, his arms wrapped tightly about himself for warmth.

The prince got up and dragged the jacket in his mouth to where Miles lay. He settled it back around Miles, who woke up and rubbed his eyes.

"You shall be rewarded for doing me such a kindness," the prince said. "Pray, tell me who you are."

"I am Miles Hendon, at your service." Miles stood up. He motioned to the rickety table, where there was a plate of bread and cold meat set out. "Let us eat now, for surely you must be very hungry. I myself could eat a bear."

"I don't know about a bear, but do you have any chicken?" Edward asked.

Miles began to sit down when Edward stiffened.

"What's wrong? Cat got your tongue?" Miles asked.

"Cats never get *anything* from me!" Edward said.

"Then what's the matter?" Miles asked.

"Don't you know you can't eat in the presence of royalty? You must stand behind me while I eat. Only when I have finished may you eat your meal!"

"I can't sit?" Miles said. He took a moment to look the prince over. "Well, I don't mind playing along for a while."

Miles stood behind Edward's chair while the prince ate. When Edward was finished, he turned and motioned for Miles to sit. "Please, be seated and eat."

"Why, thank you, Your Majesty," Miles said. He sat at the table opposite Edward and ate. All the while, he was aware of the prince staring at him. "What is it?" Miles asked.

"You have about you a noble bearing," Edward said. "And thy clothes, though faded and ragged, are of a rich material."

"If I say my father was a baronet, a member of royalty, you'll think I am as mad as people think you are."

"Tell me thy story," Edward said, "for I shall believe thee. I know all too well what it is like for people to think you are not who you are."

"Well," said Miles, "my father is Sir Richard of Hendon Hall."

"Hendon Hall!" exclaimed Edward. "That sounds vaguely familiar."

Miles nodded. "I was betrayed by my brother, who sought the fortune of the woman I loved," he said. "He persuaded my father to banish me. They forced me to leave the household for three years so that he might marry my Edith. He wanted her money, not her love. So I was banished. While I was gone, I was taken captive in a war and held in a foreign prison for seven long years. Now my banishment is over, and surely my family must think me dead. I have to make my way back to Hendon Hall and the woman I love."

Edward stood up. "That's like me—trying to get back to your rightful home!" He smiled. "You saved me from injury and shame. You saved my life. I can now help you. I will right thee! For I am the prince of Wales, to be crowned king on Thursday!"

Miles Hendon bowed. "If you want to be called 'Your Majesty,' I will call you 'Your Majesty,' because I like you." He bowed deeply. "Perhaps we shall right our wrongs together."

"Do you wish anything else in return?" the prince said. "To be an earl? A duke? All the food you can eat?"

Miles laughed. "I suppose I could ask for anything, now, couldn't I?" he said.

"Anything," Edward agreed. "A life of luxury . . . a castle . . . anything."

Miles stroked his chin. "Thinking on it, what I really would like is to be able to sit at the table and eat at the same time as the prince."

The prince was silent for a moment and deep in thought.

"Is it too much of a thing to ask?" Miles inquired.

The prince studied Miles, then grandly lifted his front paw. "That is not such a large favor to ask, not after how you have protected me. Thy petition is granted!"

"Thank goodness!" Miles said joyfully.

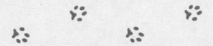

Thank goodness Edward had found himself a friend. Everybody needs a best friend—just like the way Joe has me. But what is Tom doing for some creature comfort? Let's take a look and see.

Chapter Ten

Wishbone could see it all now—*he* was the pauper. He was pacing in the prince's grand room at the palace. He was so lonely, however, that he was practically sitting up and begging for companionship!

Tom was worrying over his situation in the palace. It was Tuesday—one day closer to his coronation. There didn't seem to be a single thing he could do about it. No one believed he wasn't the prince. He was sure that once the royal household found out the truth, he would be locked up in a dungeon forever—held without food, water, or squeak toys! Already that morning, the royal tailor had come in and fitted him for a special robe to wear during the coronation. Although Tom had fussed and growled and kept moving his tail so the fit would not be right, the tailor had not given up until he had finished his task.

Tom kept imagining what it would feel like when the golden crown was placed on his head. He saw it coming nearer and nearer. It didn't take much imagination at all to feel how heavy it would be. It might weigh him down in more ways than he could guess. He knew that he didn't want to be king at all, held captive in a castle with strict rules to follow, and bone-headed orders to give. He wanted his own house, his own clothes—and his own bone! But no one would listen to him when he insisted that he was Tom Canty the pauper. Every time he opened his chamber door to escape, six gentlemen servants and two pages bowed before him and whispered, "The prince! The prince!"

"A cat may have nine lives, but I seem to have two

to deal with now—my own, and the prince's—one life too many! I surely need a friend!" Tom cried.

Just then, as if in answer to his prayers, a young lad came into his chamber.

"Who is this?" the pauper asked.

"Why, surely thou remembers me. I am your whipping boy, Humphrey Marlow," the boy replied.

"My *what*? My *whipping* boy?" Tom was astonished.

"Why, yes. When you get your lessons wrong, I'm the one who takes the blame."

"But why should you take punishment meant for me?" asked the pauper, aghast.

Humphrey looked at Tom as if he had gone even madder than before. "Sire, it wouldn't be proper to punish a prince. None may strike the prince with blows; therefore, I am the one to take them."

"Boy," the pauper said, "I sure wish I had someone like you around when there was that business about the chewed furniture." He studied Humphrey, who was small and frail-looking, and hardly seemed as if he could bear a single blow, let alone many.

"But I can't let you be whipped!" he cried.

"But that is my livelihood, and if you don't allow it, then my family and I shall go hungry." Humphrey looked so miserable that the pauper quickly reassured him.

"All right, all right, we'll figure something out," insisted the pauper.

Tom wasn't at all sure what to do. He knew only

that he was lonely. If he didn't find a friend soon, he might start baying at the moon. Humphrey could be that friend. Plus, Humphrey knew about court life and being a prince. Surely, Humphrey could tell him things he needed to know in order to act like Edward. He could buy him some time until the real Edward came back.

Tom brightened and motioned to the whipping boy. "Do you think I'm mad?" he asked.

Humphrey looked confused. "I'm not allowed to say, sire. It would be disrespectful, I'm afraid."

"Well," said Tom, "my memory fails me these days. If you could but be of little help to me—perhaps you could remind me of things . . . just a little . . . now and again. I never know what to say. I feel kind of muzzled."

"I would help thee with my life," said Humphrey. "I will help in thy cure!"

"And I will help you by making sure you are not beaten and that you keep your job!"

The two talked about a prince's life at court, and what it was that a prince did there.

"You get up early and walk in the royal gardens," Humphrey said. "You take fencing lessons and music lessons, and study Greek, which you don't like."

"Right," said Tom, pretending to know what Humphrey was talking about. He hesitated. "And in the afternoon, I play fetch with the servants?"

Humphrey laughed.

"Just joking," Tom said quickly. "I meant that in the afternoon I sign petitions."

Humphrey nodded.

"I do!" Tom said, excited at getting one thing correct about court life. "I really do!" Tom smiled. "Do I ever talk to the common people?"

"Sometimes one or two might be brought before you with a request."

"That's good," Tom said thoughtfully. "A prince should talk with his subjects."

Humphrey told him more about how he spent his day. After a while, the pauper began to feel better. Not only did he think he might act more like a prince and save himself until the real prince returned, but he believed he might actually be good at it! He was sad when the boy said it was time for him to leave.

"Tell me about the coronation," Tom said. "Does anyone ever call it off?"

"Call it off?" Humphrey echoed, confused. "Why would that ever happen?"

"Well . . ." Tom floundered. "You know, if it's a rainy, gloomy day—you don't want a coronation on a miserable day like that, right?"

"Oh, I don't think the people care about that," Humphrey said.

"Well, I care," Tom insisted. "As prince, I say I won't be crowned king on a rainy day." He brightened again, perking up his ears. "And . . . and as prince, I say I won't be crowned if it's too sunny, either."

Humphrey shook his head. "I don't think anything can stop the coronation—not even a prince."

Tom felt his spirits deflating and his tail drooped.

Humphrey got ready to leave, bowing before the pauper.

"You really have to go? Will you come back?" Tom asked Humphrey hopefully. He scooted closer to Humphrey. He gave the boy an encouraging lick on his hand. "Next time, can we play?"

Humphrey looked confused for a moment. "Play?" he repeated.

"Yes—you know . . . fetch, hide the bone, find the bone, eat the bone. Whatever." Tom looked hopeful.

Humphrey bowed deeply. "You are the prince of Wales," he said. "Your every wish is my command. If you wish it, I shall return."

"I do, indeed!" Tom said happily. He wagged his tail good-bye to Humphrey as the boy left. "Come back soon!" he called. "Don't make me sit up and beg!"

He watched Humphrey leave and thought of Edward again. "Edward, you come back soon, too!" he cried.

Chapter Eleven

Wishbone imagined that he was Prince Edward, warming his whiskers and snuggled down in his new friend Miles's humble apartment. The safety and the food were really something he could get his teeth around. Edward was still just as anxious, though, to return to the palace life as the little pauper Tom was to leave it. He just had to get back there before it was too late for either one of them!

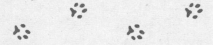

That Tuesday, while Miles fell back asleep and Tom was being fitted for a coronation robe, the prince kept thinking about the palace. He was the one who was supposed to be crowned king—not the pauper! He began to fear he might never see the palace again. *I need a walk to unleash a plan or two,* Edward thought. He trotted out into the cool air and felt the wind ruffling his fur. Suddenly, he was grabbed up by the scruff of his neck by John Canty!

"So you think you can escape your own father!" John Canty said angrily.

"Unhand me! You're not my father!" the prince cried. "I'm going to nip this in the bud—or at least nip this in the John Canty!" he said. He snapped his jaws at John Canty, who immediately smacked him.

"Oh, I'm not your father, aren't I? We'll just see about that! You're coming with me, and you're going to steal!" John Canty cried. "You will give a command performance."

"Wait! Can't we discuss this?" Edward pleaded. "I know about commands. Tell me to sit or roll over, but not to steal!"

John Canty ignored him and tightened his hold.

"Stop! Unhand me! Where are you taking me?" the prince demanded.

"You'll soon find out," John Canty warned. He dragged the prince to a clearing deep in the forest. A pack of thieves were warming themselves around a fire.

The poor little prince surveyed his muddy, torn paws. "Boy, this isn't exactly Buckingham Palace!" he said.

The men around the campfire were ragged-looking, dressed in tattered, dirty clothing. They were covered with equally dirty blankets. They did not look upon the little prince with any kindness or interest.

John Canty hurled the prince down among them.

"Sit, Your Highness," he said with a sneer, "and meet your loyal subjects!"

The men all looked over at Edward and laughed at him.

"Get warm," John Canty ordered. "Then get ready to steal!"

The prince moved closer to the fire. He had no weapons to defend himself, and he was so tired that he doubted his bark could carry farther than the edge of the camp. The men associated with John Canty looked mean to him. Edward was glad enough that they ignored him for the most part. Swapping stories, drinking great gulps of ale, they laughed and talked.

"I was once a farmer," said one man with a great black patch over his left eye. "I had a loving wife and child. When my wife nursed a sick man and he died, she was burned as a witch."

The prince leaned forward, astonished, his whiskers lifting up. *This cannot be!* he thought.

"Then my child took sick and I had no money, but I begged the doctor to give her some medicine. When he wouldn't give it to me, I stole it. I ended up in the stockade. My little one died while I was held in prison and beaten. Oh, how I curse English law!" he shouted.

Another one of the thieves shook his head. "Everyone knows it's a crime to be hungry in England."

"Everyone knows what being poor in England will get you!" one of the thieves said.

"A hanging!" someone cried. "A beating!"

"Burning at the stake!" another said.

The prince felt his heart swell with compassion and his fur bristle with rage. "I am Edward, soon to be king of England. When I get back to court, I'll see that the laws are changed!"

"You!" hooted one of the thieves. "Why would you help us men?"

"I'm the king," Edward said. "I'm royalty, and I will be a best friend to all men."

"Ignore him, he's mad," John Canty said.

"Am I foaming at the mouth? Am I going round and round chasing my tail? I'm not mad!" the prince cried. "I tell you, I'm to be the king of England!"

The thieves were more inclined to listen to John Canty than to what they considered crazy ravings.

They paid Edward no mind, going on with their drinking and storytelling. Then they began to get up.

"Come on now!" John Canty cried, dragging the prince to his feet. "We have places to go and people to rob!" He boxed Edward on his ears, hitting him soundly with the palms of both his hands. "You're coming with us, like it or not!"

I like it as much as a flea bath! Edward thought. *Will this nightmare never end?* He thought of the pauper, about to be crowned. Then he thought of his other friend, Miles Hendon, who said he would protect the prince. "Oh, where are both of you now?" he cried.

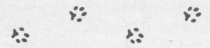

The troop made their way out of the clearing and went into London. It was a small enough city, with a few shops set up, and a fair amount of people milling about with parcels. There was a buzz of excitement. At one point Edward heard someone mention the coronation. A woman in a fur-lined bonnet exclaimed, "I'll have to buy a new hat. I'd give anything to see the king!"

"He's right in front of you!" Edward cried out, attracting the woman's attention.

"Pay him no mind, he's crazy!" John Canty bellowed.

The woman frowned at Edward. "You, a king!" She laughed. "Be gone, beggar!"

She's right, Edward thought in misery. *Look at me!*

Burrs, ticks, matted fur! Still, he kept thinking, he had to get back to the palace by Thursday, the very day of the coronation!

I had better keep my eyes and ears open and my nose on alert, Edward thought.

John Canty shoved Edward over to a corner of the road by an ale house. "Steal!" he commanded.

"I told you—I'm not going to steal!" Edward cried.

"Fine. Then you'll have to act as a decoy so we can do the stealing. You just stand there and look pitiful," John Canty commanded. "If I see you even wink or try to give our plans away, I'll beat you so badly you won't be able to stand up for days!"

So, poor little Edward stood shivering in the cold. *I'd be a lot warmer if I hadn't shed so much from nerves,* he thought. He didn't have to pretend to look pitiful—he *was* pitiful.

Soon a wealthy-looking gentleman in a tall hat approached him. "Please, take this," the man said, offering Edward some coins. Edward didn't move, but the man pressed the money onto the ground in front of Edward. As the man bent, John Canty suddenly crept forward behind him. Carefully, John Canty lowered his hand down into the gentleman's coat. Slowly, slowly, he lifted up his hand again, revealing a fat wallet. He winked at Edward as he pocketed the wallet. Quickly, he stepped back, just as the fine gentleman stood up straight again. "I wish you good luck," the man said to Edward, tipping his hat, then going on his way.

"Good work!" John Canty said when the man had walked away.

Edward felt miserable. "I'm not doing that again!" he proclaimed, but John Canty was busy counting the money and ignored him.

"When will this end?" Edward asked himself. "I can't bear much more of it!"

That night, while the troop slept, Edward made his escape. He ran from the city, through the outlying fields, as fast as his four legs would carry him. He panted so hard that his tongue was hanging out. Finally, by Wednesday morning, he came to a small, white-painted farmhouse. Exhausted, his tail drooping, he stumbled into the kitchen.

There was a long wooden table and four chairs. A bowl of flowers sat on the table. A woman with long dark hair and a blue dress was cooking something in an iron pot over an inviting-looking fire. It smelled so delicious that the prince thought he might swoon with hunger. The woman smiled at him. "Well, look what the cat dragged in," she said, but her voice was pleasant.

"Cat? What cat?" The prince looked around. "I'm allergic to cats. They carry fleas and germs. They scratch everything. There's also something mighty fishy about their food."

"Who might you be?" the woman inquired.

"I am the next king of England." Edward tried to draw himself up so he might look a little regal. He was so tired he couldn't help but lean against the wall. It made him appear smaller and weaker than ever before.

The woman laughed. "Well," she said. "Then I can hardly feed you leftovers, the way I do with the other beggars who come around here. If you're to be the king, I'll have to make an exception, won't I?"

"Leftovers sound mighty tasty to me," Edward said with enthusiasm.

She set a plate of stew on the table and pulled out a chair. The prince was overwhelmed by her simple kindness. When she sat down, he made an exception to his rule of not eating with commoners. He sat down as well. The two had an excellent meal of stew. When they finished eating, the prince even offered to do the dishes.

"These dishes look practically fresh the way you've licked them clean," the woman said. She was gracious about allowing Edward to do the dishes, even though he did not do such a good job of it.

"A king should know what his subjects do," Edward told himself. He was about to finish washing when he heard John Canty's voice. Terrified, he turned tail and ran out the back way.

"Where are you going?" the woman called after him, but the prince kept running. What a lucky break for him that he did, because he ran right into the arms of Miles Hendon—and rescue!

Yikes! The terrific twosome is back in action! Let's hope they can get to the palace in time. But who is going to rescue the pauper? My fur is standing on end just thinking about it.

Chapter Twelve

Wishbone fantasized that he was the pauper. It was now Wednesday, the day before the coronation. All Tom could think about was how time was running out—faster than even his four legs could carry him!

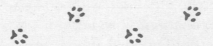

The morning before he was to be crowned king, the terrified pauper was led once again into a great room with many windows. There were even more courtiers whose sole function seemed to be nothing more than to stand about and watch him. Lord Hertford instructed the pauper in the signing of sheets and sheets of official papers and in meeting and greeting the dignitaries and courtiers. Tom continued to try to figure out what it was he was supposed to do. Every once in a while he looked longingly out the window. He yearned for the outdoor life he had once lived.

When he gathered his courage, he tapped Lord Hertford on the shoulder with one paw. "So, what about this coronation?" he said.

Lord Hertford nodded at him. "Anxious, are you? It will be here soon enough."

Either way, Tom was doomed. He would either succeed in being so princelike that the royal household would think he was Edward—and then he would be trapped as king—or he would fail, and they might throw him in the dungeon!

He was staring out the window when, in the distance, he noticed a shouting mob following a terrified peasant woman and her equally frightened young daughter. "I wish I knew what that was about," he said.

"But you're the prince," responded one of the earls. "You can find out whatever you wish."

The earl bowed before Tom. "Your Majesty," he said, "do I have your permission to act on your request?"

Tom thought for a moment. These people had to do what he commanded, just as if they were in obedience school!

"Oh, gladly, yes, do find out. Perhaps being a king isn't so dreary, after all," said Tom.

A messenger was quickly dispatched to find out the source of the commotion, while Tom waited. The messenger returned almost immediately. He told Tom that the woman and her daughter were witches, on their way to execution.

Tom felt a whine of sympathy lodge deep in his belly. His tail drooped in compassion. "Witches!" Tom exclaimed. He had heard of such people. "Where are their tall black hats?" he asked. "What about their big black cats?" Although he knew witches were supposed to be dangerous, he couldn't help wanting actually to *see* one. "They don't look like witches to me."

"Looks aren't everything," Lord Hertford said.

"Speak for yourself," said Tom, admiring his own well-groomed reflection in the window. "Bring them here so that I may get a *better* look at them!" Tom commanded. He was stunned and thrilled when the messenger obeyed instantly. *Why, I could get used to this, perhaps,* Tom thought.

The two terrified creatures were brought before Tom. They kneeled, sobbing and shivering. "Have mercy!" the woman cried, wringing her hands. "My girl is just a little thing! Have mercy!" She wrapped her arms around her daughter. The little girl cowered and hid within the folds of her mother's ragged clothes.

"What did they do?" Tom asked.

"They sold themselves to the devil!" cried one of the royals. "They caused a storm to brew just by taking off their stockings!"

The pauper looked at the woman in amazement. "A storm! I'm not that big on storms. Fur has its charms, but it's not always waterproof, you know," said Tom. "Have you always been able to create storms when you take off your stockings?"

"They'll burn for what they have done!" Lord Hertford cried.

The pauper drew himself up. It was a cruel law that would burn a mother and her child. *If I ever see Edward again, I'll tell him to change the law allowing such a terrible act,* Tom thought. Then he remembered that everyone thought *he* was Edward. He could change the law himself right that very second. This was his chance to do more than merely look and act like royalty—this was his chance to do some good.

"I am the prince of Wales, am I not?" he said as he looked at the courtiers standing nearby. Around him people nodded. "My wish is thy command, right? I say 'heel' or 'fetch' or 'stay' and you guys do it. That's what you all said, right?"

More nods. Tom thought carefully about what was fair.

"Okay," he said, then turned to the woman. "If thou art truly a witch, exert thy power! I would see a storm!"

"Your Highness!" The courtiers all ducked for cover.

The poor woman wept. "I have been falsely accused, oh, my lord. I have not the power to do such a thing."

"Please. Cause the storm and thee and thy child shall go free and blameless."

"Really? You will set my child free?"

"My word is good," Tom promised.

The whole court hushed as the woman sat down. Slowly, she took off her stockings.

Tom looked around. "No storm yet," he said.

The woman then began to take off the little girl's stockings. Several royals hid their heads and looked around for shelter, but still there was no storm. The woman put the stockings on the floor.

The pauper looked around. The room was still and quiet and very, very dry.

"It's not exactly raining cats and dogs, now, is it?" Tom said. "More's the pity, because I could use the company—and the chase." He waved his paws. "In any case, any mother, including my own, would cause heaven to rain down storms to save her child—even if that child was the runt of the litter. This woman clearly loves her daughter, and therefore she is surely blameless. I give my command to let them go!" he insisted.

"What a merciful man," someone whispered. A low buzz of admiration swept through the crowd in the room.

I knew I could be a good prince, Tom thought, beaming. *I just knew it! But that doesn't mean I want the job permanently!*

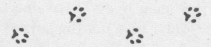

So here is a bit of presto-changeo! The pauper is becoming quite a prince of a fellow! The prince is opening his eyes to the poverty and the misery in his kingdom and is vowing to do something about the horrible circumstances. . . . That reminds me— it looks as though Joe is about to really learn the score himself in the Tigers–Banshees game. I'm just the dog to help him.

Chapter Thirteen

Wishbone paced the stands, his nails clicking on the wood. He watched Mr. King wave his notebook angrily at Joe. "Rudeness is really at the top of *my* list of pet peeves!" Wishbone said. "Why can't he just let Joe try to do his job?"

Mr. King didn't seem as if he wanted to listen to Wishbone or Joe or anyone else. "Why don't you just stay out of my way? I'll get you out of this mess," Mr. King said to Joe.

Joe drew himself up. "Uh . . . sir . . . I appreciate your concern, but I can handle this."

"I don't like the looks of this one bit," Ellen said to Wanda.

"Let's go down there and see what's going on," said Mrs. Barnes.

The three of them stood up and started making their way down the stands.

"Wait for us!" David said, getting up with Sam.

"And the dog! Don't forget the dog!" Wishbone

said, scampering down after them. "Free from this exile at last!" he said.

The group made their way across the field, led by Wishbone. "Yea, the gang's all here!" Wishbone cried with joy. "Just in time, too, because it sure looks as if Joe could use a cheering squad. Come on, guys! Joe! Joe! Hoo-ray!"

Mrs. Barnes went over to Joe and settled her hand on his shoulder. "How's it going? Having fun?" She looked at Joe, who seemed miserable, and then at Mr. King, who appeared to be furious. Her own face suddenly filled with concern. "Is everything okay?"

"Well, judging from that scoreboard, I would say things are far from okay," Mr. King said. "Seventeen to twenty in favor of the Banshees isn't exactly what I'd call a cause for celebration. I don't know why a *real* coach wasn't hired for this game." He waved one hand loftily at Joe. "Just because you wear the hat doesn't mean you're really a coach. Why, you're just a . . . a . . . a pretender to the throne."

"Wait a minute! That's not fair!" Wishbone said, barking.

Mr. King looked down at him. "What's this dog doing here on the field? Is that sanitary?"

"I beg your pardon," said Wishbone, drawing himself up.

"What a way to run a game," said Mr. King.

Ellen shook her head in anger. "Look, buster, I don't know who you think you are, but—"

Wanda touched Ellen on the shoulder. "Don't lose your temper," she advised. "That's all they ever want. Come on, let's go back to the stands."

Ellen, Sam, and David followed Wanda back to their seats. Joe walked closer to first base, with Mr. King following.

Wishbone looked sympathetically at Joe. He glanced around the field. "I've got to help Joe. Let's take inventory here. What can I do? I can look cute. That always helps. I can bark." He stared out at the game, where Emily was ready to bat. "And from where I stand, this team could use a first-base coach. That's it! That's what I'll do!"

He ran to first base.

"Yoo-hoo! Girls! Look who's here!" Wishbone raced over to first base and positioned himself there, right where all the Tigers could see him.

Emily was at bat. She smiled at Wishbone. "I'm going to get you, Wishbone," she crooned. She leaned over the plate and whacked the ball!

"Run!" Wishbone called. Emily raced over to Wishbone. "Come on, sweetie!" Wishbone shouted. "For the sake of the game, I'm yours!" Wishbone turned around and he saw that Emily had made it to first base!

"Don't stop now!" Wishbone cried. "We've got more bases to run!" Wishbone ran to second base, turning to make sure Emily was behind him. "Hey, Joe!" he called. "How am I doing?" He turned for a second to see Joe's astonished look of delight.

Wanda suddenly jumped up. She began cheering and pointing excitedly as Wishbone led Emily to a home run.

"Good girl!" Wishbone said to Emily. He let her hug him. Then he ran over to Joe.

"Wishbone!" Joe said. "You're a great coach!"

"Who's that up next?" Sam asked.

Joe glanced toward home plate. "That's Carol. She's really shy, but she's improved her game."

"Improved! Improved isn't good enough!" said Mr. King.

"I know she can do it," Joe said. "I just know it."

"Oh, you do, do you?" said Mr. King. "You mean to tell me it's all up to her? Why, she can't even hold the bat properly! Look at her! She doesn't look like a player!"

"Well, she is," said Joe. "And she's playing." He studied Carol. "Don't forget. Move closer to the ball and swing hard."

Carol picked up the bat cautiously. She looked at the other Tigers, who rolled their eyes at her. She moved closer to the ball.

"Great. There goes the game," said Mr. King.

"Give her a chance," Wishbone said.

"Take your time, Carol!" Joe called. "You can do it!"

"I had better get back to first base," Wishbone

said. "See you guys later!" He ran over to first base and jumped around until he caught Carol's attention. "Come on, Carol!" Wishbone encouraged. He leaped into the air and did a tumble. "Hi, Carol! I'm really cute, huh?"

Carol swung as hard as she could. She hit the ball!

"She did it! She did it!" Wishbone cried.

Carol looked stunned.

"This is a job for a master coach!" Wishbone said. "Oh, Carol," he called, "do you want to pet me? Well, then come and get me!" He raced around the plates, Carol at his heels. "Come on, Carol! I am one hot dog!"

Wishbone slid into home plate, with Carol right behind him.

"Yee-haw!" crowed Wishbone. "This is what you call team coaching! Look at this!" Wishbone said. "Look at the scoreboard! Twenty-one to twenty, in favor of the Tigers! The Tigers win!" Wishbone flipped in the air. Fans poured from the stands to crowd around the winning team. "No pictures, please," said Wishbone, modestly bowing his head. "Well, maybe only a few, and remember, I have no bad side. Say 'cheese,' and lots of it!"

The Tigers bent and hugged Wishbone. Then they gathered around Carol. "I think I'm going to be sick," Carol said, panting from her run.

The other Tigers hugged her. "You're a great teammate!" they said. "Next time you can be up first!"

"We won!" Wishbone cried.

Mr. King nodded at Joe. "Well, maybe I was wrong

about Carol . . . and about you, too," he said reluctantly. "But next time, put my Katie up with the starting lineup and you could do even better."

"And what about me? Weren't you wrong about me?" Wishbone said.

Sam patted Joe on the shoulder. "Wishbone really came through for you."

"I'll say so!" said Joe. He bent down and gave Wishbone a hug.

"No false modesty here. I know I'm the greatest thing ever to walk on four legs!" Wishbone proclaimed proudly.

"But you did pretty well yourself," Wanda said. "So how does it feel now that your coaching days are over?"

Joe sighed. "It's a big, big relief."

"See, and you thought you bit off more than you could chew!" Wishbone said.

Speaking of biting off more than you can chew—which, by the way, has never been a particular problem of mine—Miles and young Edward are about to dig up even *more* troubles for themselves. This *could* keep them from getting to the palace on time! Hold on, because we're just about at the tail end of our story!

Chapter Fourteen

Wishbone wagged his tail. Suddenly he was head over paws into the story again. This time, he imagined himself as Edward, clasped tightly against his friend Miles!

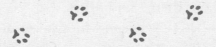

It was difficult to say who was more delighted to have found whom—the frightened Edward, or the once noble adventurer. Miles swooped Edward up in a hearty embrace.

"At last we're together again!" Miles said with great joy and relief.

"Thank goodness I found you!" Edward cried, his whole body wagging with happiness. "I didn't know who to call for help—the guards . . . or the Animal Rescue League!"

"Come on, then. We'll go to Hendon Hall and

then on to the palace. You'll see, everything is going to be all right now," Miles promised.

"Wait a minute!" Edward said. "As top dog around here, I say we go to the palace first. Thursday is the coronation."

"Today is only Wednesday! We have more than enough time!" said Miles, his eyes brimming with excitement. "Hendon Hall is on the way, and it is something to feast your eyes on!" He smiled at Edward. "And our stomachs! Wait until you taste the roasted meats. Hendon Hall is famous for them! The breads and cheeses are divine, too."

Edward felt his stomach grumbling. "Cheese, you said? Well, a short stop couldn't hurt—" Edward decided. "And it *is* along the way."

"Come on, then," said Miles.

Edward had never seen Miles so excited.

During the entire journey to the village where Hendon Hall was located, Miles couldn't stop talking about the upcoming meeting he would have there. "I shall be reunited with Edith, the woman I love!"

The village was green and pretty. Before them was a beautiful park in which Edward ached to dig. In the midst of the park was a large house with massive columns supporting it, and a great wood door with a shiny brass knocker.

Miles bowed to Edward. "Welcome to Hendon

Hall," he said. "We will knock and give my family a chance to let me reclaim peacefully what is mine. My father and the Lady Edith will be wild with joy to see me. Perhaps enough time has passed that even my brother will be glad, as well. I'll tell them you are my friend. I am sure that they will welcome you as well. My home will be your home!"

Edward was touched by his friend's genuine devotion. Edward didn't have the heart to point out to Miles that as king, he wouldn't need anyone else's home. Instead, he licked Miles's hand. "You are too good to me," he said.

Miles knocked on the door. A young man answered, and three servants stood behind him. Miles began to laugh. "It's Hugh, my brother!" he cried. "And the servants!"

Hugh blinked. "Who are you?" he asked. The servants looked down at the floor.

"Thy brother—Miles! Don't you know me?" Then Miles looked at the servants. "And all of you who have served me for so many years, don't you recognize my face?"

"Take a good sniff," Edward urged. "I always say, 'When you're not sure who someone is, go for the scent.'"

The servants stepped back farther, keeping their heads down to the ground.

Hugh shook his head. "You must be mad. My brother Miles was reported dead, fallen in battle."

"I am proof that is a lie," Miles said. He turned to

Edward. "See? You are not the only one whose identity is held in question." He turned back to Hugh. "And where is my father? And Edith?"

"My father is dead. And Edith? Why, Edith is my wife."

Suddenly, Miles straightened. "My father is dead? And Edith is *your* wife? My Edith can't be your wife!" he cried.

"Wait a minute here. I don't know you," Hugh said. "The servants don't know you. There must be some mistake. I would thank you to leave now, before you cause any more trouble."

"Trouble? What trouble have I caused?" Miles was stunned. "There must be some mistake, indeed. But we shall return to make things right."

The door was slammed so fast and so hard that it caught Edward's tail end. "Hey!" Edward yelped, freeing himself and surveying his tail, which had lost a bit of fur. "Little things mean a lot!"

During the entire trip back to town, Miles was silent. "I know just how you feel," Edward told him, heeling beside him. Miles could not be comforted, not even when they were sitting down to a hot dinner at a local inn, where they warmed themselves in front of a fire.

"Things will right themselves," Miles said. Just then the door flew open and two officers stormed in, surrounding Miles and Edward.

"You both are under arrest!" they cried. "On orders of the master of Hendon Hall!"

"For what?" Miles cried as the officers grabbed him.

"For disturbing the peace of the master of Hendon Hall. And for lying."

"Arrested!" cried Edward. "You can't arrest me! I'm to be crowned king!" The guards refused to listen. They slapped him roughly until he was terrified into silence. Edward, shackled to his friend, and dragged by guards, was white with fear. "I'm to go to prison? Treated like a stray when I have a pedigree?" Edward cried, panicking. "How can such a thing be?" He bared his teeth, but he was too frightened to growl.

"Don't worry," Miles told him. "I said I would protect thee, and I shall!"

Miles and Edward were soon thrown into a large, crowded room in a damp and dirty prison, and they were chained to a wall. The only warmth that they had were two very soiled and tattered prison blankets. "Never have I seen such a place!" Edward cried, his ears pinning back in alarm.

The room was filled with young women, children, and very old men.

"What have you done that you should be here?" Edward asked. "You don't look criminal or fierce or dangerous in any way to me."

"I stole bread for my child," one woman answered. "But in the end it didn't matter, because she died anyway."

"I was accused of witchcraft," said another. "The neighbor's cow died, and I was held responsible for it. So I must hang."

Edward was so angry that he couldn't help but bare his teeth. "No one believes I am the prince! But when I get back to the palace, I am going to change these terrible laws! Maybe it wasn't so bad to be placed in prison. Now I know about how my subjects suffer!"

All that night, Edward couldn't sleep. He lay against Miles, the two of them hugging each other for warmth.

The next day, Thursday, Edward and Miles had their trial—and they were not pardoned at all. As luck would have it, their trial was as clipped as the summer cut on a poodle. Edward was sentenced to spend time in the stockade. He put his tail between his legs and whimpered.

Miles spoke in his friend's defense. "Let the lad go! Can't you see how frail he is?"

"Will you take his blows for him, then—as well as your own?" the guard standing outside asked.

"That I will!" Miles cried.

"No! Don't do that!" Edward yelped.

The prince listened as Miles was led away to the stockade and given six lashes. Edward cried at the sound of each and every blow. Even though his own tender hide and fur were not pierced by the fierce sting

119

of the whip, he still felt the lashes paining him as much as they hurt his friend.

When the beating was finished, Edward joined Miles and embraced him. He licked at his friend's wounds. "Old family recipe," Edward said. "You'll feel better in two shakes of a tail." He soothed his friend some more. "I'll make you an earl for showing such kindness to me."

When Miles was released from prison, he ignored Edward's pleas to head for the palace. Miles began walking away from the prison toward Hendon Hall.

"The coronation!" Edward cried. He tried to nudge Miles in the other direction, toward the palace. "It's today. We can still make it!"

"No, I must settle this now!" Miles insisted. He strode farther into town, Edward lagging behind.

Suddenly, a band of pickpockets surrounded and separated them. "Miles!" cried Edward. He nipped at the pickpockets, chomping his teeth and struggling to get away. "Miles!" he called. When he at last escaped from the pickpockets, he found that he was alone.

Edward began walking toward the palace. The closer he got, the more anxious he became. Would he be too late and be forever lost in the underbelly of London? Would he ever find his friend Miles again?

The coronation clock is ticking!

Chapter Fifteen

Wishbone imagined himself as Tom. He was sleeping restlessly in his bed, his tail curled beneath him. He hoped that he would find that the coming coronation was just a dream.

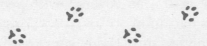

"Wake up, Your Highness," Lord Hertford said. "Today is the day!"

Tom felt his fur stand on end. It was Thursday! The coronation! He didn't know what to do, except that he couldn't be crowned king. "Listen," he said, "I'm not the king!"

"Of course you aren't right now. But you will be," Lord Hertford said. He clapped his hands and the door opened. Twenty servants entered the room, bowing to Tom. In back of them was a man carrying a great robe of rich gold silk trimmed with magnificent feathers.

"Here is the royal tailor, sire," Lord Hertford said, "with the ceremonial robe you were fitted for."

"I've grown too fat for it," Tom insisted. "We should put off the coronation while I diet. Nothing but milk and maybe a sprinkling of kibble for me."

Lord Hertford took up the robe and lifted it over Tom's head.

"Wait!" Tom cried.

"It's a perfect fit," Lord Hertford declared. "Come now, we don't want to be late for the procession."

Oh, yes, we do, Tom thought, but he kept silent.

Tom, Lord Hertford, and nearly a hundred servants were led out of the palace, across the grounds to the river, and onto a great white boat. Soon Tom found himself to be among a floating pageant along the river Thames. The boat was covered with red and white roses, their perfume so overpowering that Tom thought he might faint. There were great arches made of flowers for the ship to pass under. Along the riverbanks was a brilliant spectacle of fireworks exploding in the sky. People lined the way and waved and cheered. Every once in a while, he could hear someone wishing him well. He stared into the crowd and actually saw some of the people he knew from Offal Court. Although he waved furiously at them, they lowered their eyes, just as if he were really Edward.

"They don't recognize me!" Tom moaned.

"Good health and long life!" people shouted. "May you rule forever!"

May I never *rule,* Tom kept thinking. He scanned

the crowd. *There's still time for Edward to show up,* he thought hopefully.

All of London had turned out to cheer Tom on, but he felt sicker and sicker. Just then twelve servants approached him. Each one of them carried a golden bucket of shiny coins. They set the buckets at Tom's feet. For a moment, Tom thought the money was meant for him, but then he hesitated. Luckily, Lord Hertford reached down for a handful and flung it into the cheering crowd. Tom noticed that the lord threw the coins closer to the finely dressed people than to those in tatters. *That doesn't seem fair! They don't need the coins!* Tom thought. He bent and grabbed a few coins in his paws and searched the crowd for the poorest-looking of the lot. He spotted a ragtag family, their clothing filthy, their hair matted, and he flung the coins right at them. They bent, grabbed for the money, then stood and cheered him. "Long live the king!" they cried.

I'm doing some good again, Tom thought. Lord Hertford bent to grab some more coins, but Tom stopped him with his front paws.

"No, let me," he insisted. He scattered the rest of the coins into the crowd. He aimed carefully so that the youngest and the oldest and the poorest-looking people might gain a little wealth. Although the crowd was deliriously happy, Tom still couldn't keep a sad expression from his face. He still couldn't keep his tail from drooping down between his hind legs.

"Your Highness," said Lord Hertford, "the people

heard of what you did with the witches and they love you for your mercy. And I'm sure they love you for your coins. But the crowd needs to see you happy or they will think something is amiss." He pointed to a magnificent building up ahead. "There is Westminster Abbey, where you shall be crowned. Already, the gallery is filled to capacity. People have been waiting hours for a seat there to see something they may never see again in their lives—a coronation!"

Oh, I wanted to see that, too, Tom thought, *but a real coronation, with the real prince!*

Tom grew so desperate that he decided to try one last time to convince Lord Hertford of his real identity. "I'm not the prince of Wales—" he said to Lord Hertford.

The lord just gave him a look. "What, is your madness upon you again? Pray, gather your wits about you."

"Long live King Edward of England!" someone cried.

Finally, the great boat docked. Tom and all his servants were led in a grand procession toward Westminster Abbey. Torches of every color lined the streets. Inside, the abbey was strewn with diamonds and filled with so many people that it made Tom dizzy. He wagged his tail halfheartedly as the crowd rose to its feet and cheered. Everyone was straining for a glimpse of him. The air was filled with the aroma of incense, and a triumphant peal of music burst forth. The robed heads of the church began to file in. They stood on a great jeweled platform at the front of the abbey.

Tom grew paler and paler. His nose, usually so nicely cold, sweated, and his fur felt dry to the touch. He was led up to the platform and toward the blue-velvet-covered throne. All the while the crowd was cheering so loudly that he tried to fold back his ears so as not to hear them. *Will someone not rescue me?* he thought. *Edward, where are you?*

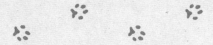

Where was Edward? Why, right in the middle of the crowd standing outside the abbey, his ears back and his tail up in determination.

"What's wrong with the king?" Edward heard someone say. "He doesn't look happy."

"Of course I'm not happy!" Edward snapped.

The person who had spoken gave him a rude look. He jostled Edward so that he fell on all four of his paws into the dirt. "I'm not talking about you!" the man said.

There was a triumphant swell of music. Edward drew close to the abbey and wagged his way inside. He stood up on his hind legs, straining to get a look. There, on the gleaming platform, right there in front of him, was the pauper! Tom Canty was trembling! He was wearing a robe of gold silk, his coat brushed to a fine sheen. The archbishop of Canterbury was lifting up the crown of England to put on Tom's head—the very same crown that belonged to no one but Edward!

"Wait! That's mine!" Edward shouted.

Chapter Sixteen

A deep hush fell over the watching crowd. It was so quiet that one could hear the fleas in Edward's fur jostling for a better position. Edward could stand it no longer. He pushed himself up on his hind legs, as high as he could go. He mustered all of his strength so that he might be heard by everyone gathered there.

"I forbid you to put the crown on his head!" Edward shouted.

In an instant, a guard seized Edward. "What is such treasonous talk?" the guard yelled. "It's prison for you!" He grabbed Edward by the scruff of his neck. He dragged him, kicking his four legs and barking, away from the abbey.

"All is lost!" Edward wailed. "I'll be thrown into that horrible prison forever now, and I'll never get out. It's worse than the pound. My father is dead, my friend Miles is gone, and I am not king! Woe is me!"

Suddenly another voice rang out.

"*He* is the king!" cried Tom Canty. "The real king! Not I! Unhand him!"

The crowd outside the abbey buzzed with confusion. "What is he saying?" people asked, gasping in surprise. "What does this mean?"

"Mind not His Majesty," Lord Hertford called out. "His madness is upon him again. Take that impostor to the dungeon!"

Tom stepped forward, panting, pushing Lord Hertford out of the way. Right there, in front of the astonished crowd, he bowed as deeply as he could to Edward. "Oh, King," he said to Edward. "I know who and what I am—I'm a mongrel. And I'm loyal above all else. So let poor Tom Canty be the first to swear loyalty to you. You should put on thy crown and walk into your own life again." He motioned for Edward to step forward. "I beg you to come and stand with me. Please."

No one would deny the king's wish, no matter how mad it seemed. The guard shoved the ragged Edward forward toward Tom, as roughly as he could.

"Long time no see," Edward said to Tom.

The two smiled at each other.

Now that the pups were side by side, the crowd suddenly began to notice the strange similarity between the two.

One of the courtiers gasped. "Why, they are like two peas in a pod! The same mouth, the same eyes! Then who is the real king, and who is the real pauper? How are we to tell if what they say is madness or the truth?"

"What is to be done?" cried an earl. "We can't crown the wrong king! But which one is he?"

Lord Hertford was deep in thought for a moment. Then he stepped forward. "As the crown's protector, I say there is only one sure test. Ask that they reproduce for us the Great Seal. Whichever of the two draws the Royal Seal correctly is the real prince!"

The Great Seal? the pauper thought. *What is the Royal Seal? Is it a big ocean animal?* He began to smile. *Why, since I haven't a clue what it is, I certainly can't draw it. Everyone will know instantly that I'm not the real prince. I'm already home, then!*

"Let's go inside. Fetch each of them a sheet of parchment," said Lord Hertford.

The prince and the pauper both went inside one of the royal chambers. Two great easels with parchment paper were put before them, along with a heavy gold quill pen.

"Gentlemen," said Lord Hertford, "begin the test. On your mark, get set—draw!"

Both the prince and the pauper drew, their heads bent over, their tails wagging in concentration. After a few moments had passed, the lord cleared his throat.

"Let us see the results." He nodded to the pauper.

"Somehow, I don't think this is what you had in mind," said the pauper as he turned his drawing around. There, covering up the whole sheet of parchment, was a great paw print. "I always sign my work," Tom said. "Here on the paper. There on the floor. You know how it is."

"And you . . ." Lord Hertford said to the prince.

The prince flipped his drawing around. There was the Great Seal in all its glory! Tom peered over to see. Edward had drawn a round circle with a pair of lions embracing in the center of it. Tom recognized the image as one of the carvings on the palace gate. "What is such a thing used for?" Tom whispered to Edward.

"When I want to make a law official, I have to stamp the parchment with this seal. Only I have the seal, and that is how people know I have made new laws."

The courtiers smiled.

"Only he who is the prince of Wales can so answer! Long live the king!" Lord Hertford cried.

"I'm free!" the pauper said gleefully.

Oh, nothing feels as good as having your old life back. Unless, of course, it's having your belly scratched—or a coronation celebration with lots of food, music . . . and more food. And the nice thing about having an imagination is that we are all invited.

The coronation festivities that evening were more splendid than anyone could have expected.

Edward, dressed in his kingly robe, fresh from his

flea bath and the royal groomer, was made king with great ceremony. Then he summoned Tom to stand before him.

"I haven't forgotten you," Edward said. "I hereby appoint you honorable king's ward. You shall always be under my protection wherever you may roam. May you have a life of comfort and dignity and honor—and all the bones you can eat! May you remember your service here with pride."

"May it please Your Majesty. Thank you," said the pauper. "That sounds delicious!"

"And," said the prince, "I will make arrangements so you can provide for your mother and family. You'll never have to beg or steal. You'll never again have to suffer the cruelties of your father, John Canty. May you accept this in remembrance of your service on behalf of this throne." He bent and picked up a scepter shaped like a bone.

"Oh, thank you!" cried Tom.

Edward smiled. His heart felt heavy, though. There was still one thing left to be made right. That had to do with his good friend Miles. But where was he? Edward searched the crowd. Just then he heard a commotion. In a far corner, a guard was roughly pulling someone to his feet.

"Up, thou mannerless clown!" the guard shouted. "Who dares to sit in the presence of the king?"

Edward stood on his hind legs to get a better view. Suddenly his whole body wagged with excitement. There was Miles, staring at him in complete wonder.

"He not only dares to sit in the presence of the king, but I gave him permission to do so right in his own home!" Edward called out. "Touch him not!" cried Edward to the guard. "Know one and all that this is my friend and my protector, Miles Hendon. If it weren't for him, I surely would be dead."

"You're really the king?" Miles asked, astonished. "You were telling me the truth?"

Edward nodded. "Now that I am king, I do so start to honor everything I promised on my adventures," Edward said to the crowd. "I told Miles he would be an earl for taking blows meant for me—and so I do proclaim that Miles Hendon is now the earl of Kent. He shall have gold and lands, and especially my protection, as surely as he has given me his. You shall be master of Hendon Hall again. I will see that justice is done with your brother."

The kindly king smiled at his friend, who bowed deeply.

"Now at last, this event is really an occasion to celebrate for all of us!" Edward said.

And celebrate they did! Miles's evil brother, fearing punishment, did a disappearing act, abandoning Edith. Edith was at last free to marry her one true love, Miles Hendon. When Tom's father, John Canty, learned that it was indeed King Edward he had been mistreating and not his son, he feared he would be beheaded, so he took off swiftly for parts unknown. He was never heard from again! Tom and the rest of his family became feted—and petted—at court. All Tom's days, he remembered the time he had been royal. As for King Edward—well, he was one of the most compassionate and kindly rulers England had ever known. He was fond of telling the story of his adventures to his people. He always said that every king should live like his subjects so that he might understand what their life was like.

Speaking of celebrations . . . let's see what is going on at Joe's house now that the big game's won—and done!

Chapter Seventeen

Wishbone sat in the kitchen, chewing over the day's events, along with a little left-over kibble from lunch. Just in the next room, Joe's whole fan club—Ellen, Sam, David, Mrs. Barnes, Wanda, Tina, and Emily—was celebrating the big win.

"Congratulations, Joe!" Mrs. Barnes said. "I knew you could do it!"

Joe blushed. "I wasn't so sure."

"Well, I was." Ellen put one arm around her son. "You'd be surprised what you can do when you put your mind to it."

"Hear! Hear!" said Wanda, waving a slice of pizza. "Let's have a pizza toast. To Joe, a really great coach!"

Wishbone suddenly smelled the pizza they were sharing and trotted into the living room. "Here I am!" he announced. "Don't think that just because I've eaten I'm not still hungry." He lifted his nose into the air, inhaling the pizza aroma with joy.

Ellen gave Joe a hug. "Admit it, Joe," she said, "your experience wasn't that bad."

"Oh, yes, it was," Joe insisted, "but I survived."

Just then the doorbell rang. "Uh-oh," said Wishbone, "is that opportunity knocking *again?*

Joe opened the door. "Mr. Barnes!" he said. "Back from your trip!"

Mr. Barnes came into the living room. "Yup, and I must say I heard good things about your coaching."

Joe shrugged, grinning. "You did?"

"I really did," said Mr. Barnes. "Your taking my place saved the day for me. Any time you want to be coach again, you just let me know."

"I think I'm pretty happy as a player," Joe said.

"Well, that's fine, Joe," said Mr. Barnes. "But you'll never be able to think of yourself as 'just a player' anymore—not now that you've experienced how the other half lives."

"I guess you're right," Joe said.

Emily and Tina approached Joe with a colorfully decorated paper plate. Spelled out in bright red, blue, and green crayon was a saying that read: TO THE BEST COACH! Around the border of the plate were big yellow stars.

"Joe," Emily said, "we want to thank you for being the best coach ever."

"Thanks," said Joe, holding up the plate so everybody could see. "This is really beautiful, everyone."

Wishbone studied the plate and then eyed the

pizza boxes on the dining room table. "Uh . . . excuse me, girls, but didn't you forget something? Remember the first-base coach? Remember the king himself of cuteness? What about my reward?"

Tina suddenly noticed Wishbone. "And this is for Wishbone," she said, handing him a bit of pizza. "For being the best dog!"

"Oh," Wishbone said with delight, "an edible trophy!" Tina and Emily petted him as he devoured the food. "You know, this would go great with anchovies, girls," Wishbone hinted.

When Wishbone was sure all the pizza was finished, he scratched at the door.

"I know the festivities are still going on, but sometimes I'm not a real party animal," he admitted.

"There you go, Wishbone," said Joe, opening the door and letting him out.

Wishbone sniffed at the air. Passing by was a poodle being walked on a silver leash by his owner. The dog had on a pale pink jacket and pink boots, but what really attracted Wishbone was the sizable bone in its mouth. "Hmm, a stranger in our neighborhood!" Wishbone said. "I'd say it's time for a dog meet-and-greet session. The Wishbone Welcome Wagon—at your service!" He barked a "hello," but the dog ignored him, and the owner stiffened.

"Heel," said the owner.

"Hey—don't you care to share?" Wishbone called out. The poodle lifted her head, ignoring him. Wishbone couldn't take his eyes off the bone, and for one moment he wished he were that dog. "Last chance!" Wishbone barked.

The owner jerked the poodle's leash tightly, making her yelp.

"Don't! That smarts!" Wishbone said. He suddenly felt sorry for the poodle, bone or not, and he suddenly didn't feel so hungry for the bone anymore. Now, nothing seemed better than simply being who he was!

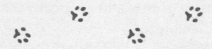

So Joe is no longer coach . . . the prince is no longer the pauper, and the pauper is no longer the prince. I bet they have all learned an important

lesson—what is called the *moral* of the story. I bet what they have all learned is that you have to walk in someone else's paws to know what someone else's life is really like. That's something to chew on! Experience sure is a great teacher, but school is out, and the next subject I want to ponder is my dinner! Despite the size of the bone that poodle was carrying, I think I'll stay who I am—at least until the next story!

About Mark Twain

When you think of Mark Twain, you might think of a gruff, cigar-smoking man with a shock of white hair and a big mustache! You might think of a man who wrote about the Mississippi River. You might also think of a man who wrote funny books that pointed out things that were wrong with society. You'd be right on all counts.

Mark Twain was born Samuel Langhorne Clemens in 1835. He first trained to be a printer, but later he took a job as a riverboat pilot on the great Mississippi. It was this job that inspired many of his greatest stories, including *Huckleberry Finn* and *Tom Sawyer*. His books were famous for being stories that could be read on many levels. For example, *Huckleberry Finn* can be read as an adventure story of a young boy and his friend floating down the river. But it is also a story about how a boy comes to realize that slavery is wrong.

Twain also had a career as a comic speaker. He traveled all over and told funny stories. Mark Twain, beloved author, produced works that have been made into countless movies.

About *The Prince and the Pauper*

Samuel Langhorne Clemens (or Mark Twain) usually wrote about what he knew best—which was his experiences as a riverboat pilot on the Mississippi, or his life out west. When he visited England in 1877, however, he became so fascinated by the country that he decided to write about it. He read lots of history books about England, and on November 23 of that year, he wrote down an idea for a novel: Edward VI and a poor young boy who happened to look just like him exchanged places! That idea soon became one of Twain's most beloved novels—*The Prince and the Pauper.*

Twain always said that he wrote the novel for the love of it. Because the book was gentler and less serious than the ones he had written before, he didn't expect it to find much of an audience, except among children. But Twain was wrong. *The Prince and the Pauper* has been delighting people of all ages for more than a hundred years, and it has even been performed onstage, and made into movies, too!

Who hasn't imagined changing places with someone else—even for just a day? Like Wishbone, any reader can be enthralled by this rousing story of mistaken identity. *The Prince and the Pauper* is a thrilling adventure and a wonderful look at what life in London was like in the sixteenth century. It's sure to make you think twice about wanting to be someone else, and to really appreciate who you are—which is someone special, indeed!

About Caroline Leavitt

Mark Twain's *The Prince and the Pauper* is one of Caroline Leavitt's favorite books—just as Wishbone is one of her favorite dogs. Writing about the two in this WISHBONE novel was certainly a great thrill for her.

An award-winning author, Caroline has written six novels, including another WISHBONE title, *Robinhound Crusoe,* which is based on Daniel Defoe's *Robinson Crusoe.* Although her other novels are written for adults, her last title, *Living Other Lives,* was named one of the best books of 1996 for teenagers by the New York City Public Library. She has also written magazine articles and screenplays.

Although Caroline has never actually traded places with another person, when she was in school she did pretend to be her older sister Ruthy on the telephone. Caroline now thinks there is nothing more exciting than being herself. She lives in a 124-year-old house with her husband, Jeff; baby son, Max; and tortoise, Minnie. They're all as one-of-a-kind like that smart, cute, and talkative dog, Wishbone!